PRIMA FACIE

BY THE SAME AUTHOR

Medicus

Terra Incognita

Persona non Grata

Caveat Emptor

Semper Fidelis

Tabula Rasa

Vita Brevis

Memento Mori

Praise for the MEDICUS series:

"...easily the best of the various detective series set during the Roman Empire..."

Morning Star

"Downie remains a peerless storyteller and a master entertainer. BBC's Masterpiece should take a long look at this series. It's a winner."

Kirkus Reviews

Human, satisfying and meticulously researched, Downie's series is always a pleasure to read. Full of wit, action and warmth.

Imogen Robertson, Historia

"Downie has a rare talent for combining great writing, razor wit and detailed historical research, and weaving them around a sharply drawn character set in a way that brings two thousand years ago into focus as clearly as if it was yesterday."

Lynne Patrick, Hey there's a dead guy in the living room"

"This is wonderful prose, laced through with wit and warmth, and it's a joy to read."

For Winter Nights, review of MEMENTO MORI

First published 2019

ISBN 978-1-9164694-8-8

PRIMA FACIE

A Crime Novella of the Roman Empire

RUTH DOWNIE

GRAMPUS

Nuptiae consistere non possunt nisi consentiant omnes, id est qui coeunt quorumque in potestate sunt.

A marriage cannot exist without the consent of all parties, that is, of those who come together, and also of those under whose authority they are.

- Julius Paulus

About this story

Roman Army medic Ruso was only meant to exist for three chapters of a "start a novel" competition. The British slave he reluctantly rescued in those chapters didn't even have a name—but when the story began to extend into a whole novel, it was clear that he couldn't keep calling her "you". Nor could he pronounce her native name. Between them, they settled on "Tilla".

Ruso and Tilla's adventures in Roman Britain and elsewhere have now filled a series of eight crime novels, and they have made friends in lands they never knew existed. Some of their friends have asked what happened between their trip to Rome in VITA BREVIS and their arrival back in Britannia in MEMENTO MORI. Did they call in to see Ruso's debt-laden family in the south of France?

Indeed they did. This is the story of that visit. Regular readers will meet some familiar faces here. Readers who have never spent time with Ruso and Tilla before will, I hope, enjoy the story without needing to know anything about what happened beforehand.

PRIMA FACIE

A NOVELLA

IN WHICH our hero, Gaius Petreius Ruso, will be...

assisted by

Tilla, his wife
Publius, a young aristocrat

accompanied by

Mara, his daughter

interrogated by

Marcia, his eldest sister

told that he is horrible by

Flora, his youngest sister

unexpectedly kissed by

Verax, boyfriend of Flora

informed by

Bushy, Wispy and Patchy, three bearded young aristocrats

saddened by

Sabinus, a local landowner
Corinna, sister of Publius the aristocrat

puzzled by

Titus, son of Sabinus the landowner

importuned by

Arria, his stepmother

confused by

Xanthe, a working girl
Too many nieces and nephews

outshone in all aspects of farming and family administration by

Lucius, his brother

1

Roman Gaul, AD123

Verax glanced at the trio of slaves lolling against the walls of the courtyard and wondered how they put up with this. Were they impatient? Bored? Angry? In the uncertain torchlight, he couldn't tell. Maybe spending a summer evening outside someone else's party was better than serving in their masters' homes. It certainly wasn't better than the plans he'd been forced to set aside himself.

He drank his share of the vinegary wine when the jug came around. A kitchen girl appeared with a tray of leftovers. After she had gone, Verax and the slaves entertained themselves by guessing what they were eating.

The laughter from the dining room grew louder. The slaves discussed where their owners would be going to escape the summer heat, and who would win the town wrestling championship: an event someone had made more interesting by setting up an illicit betting ring. Verax declined the offer to join.

He had passed some of the time by whittling the rough shape of an olive-wood hairpin for Flora, but the daylight had faded hours ago and now there was nothing to do but stand around, like the carriage horses waiting patiently in their harness to take Titus home.

There was a brief distraction when two of the young masters staggered into the courtyard and vomited over the rose beds. Their slaves abandoned a dispute about racing teams, cleaned them up, and steered them back indoors.

Verax wondered what he was missing at Flora's house. There would surely have been time to snatch a few moments alone with her before one of her small cousins barged in to ask what they were doing. Instead, here he was in town, watching rich boys throw up. And was his own young master grateful? Of course he wasn't.

Instead of thanking Verax for stepping in this evening, Titus had leaned out of the carriage window and shouted at him to get the horses moving faster. The horses had not gone faster enough, and Titus complained that at this rate the fun would be over by the time they got there.

"I don't drive often, sir," Verax had pointed out, biting back *do it yourself if you think it's so easy*. "I'm your father's wheelwright."

"I know who you are, boy. I'm not blind."

And I'm not your boy, you pampered shrimp.

None of this would have been necessary if the pampered shrimp hadn't been banned from staying in the town house after the wreckage of the last party.

Verax perched himself on the step of the carriage and yawned. "If he doesn't come out soon," he remarked, "I might just drive home to bed and leave him to walk."

There was an awkward silence in the courtyard. Someone unhooked the wine jug that had been hung over the hand of the statue of Bacchus, god of the grape harvest, and passed it across. "Have another drink."

He had embarrassed them. Whatever the slaves

thought of the young men who routinely left them waiting for hours in the dark, they weren't going to say it out loud. Perhaps because they were loyal. Perhaps because you never knew who might be listening, and who might spill your unwise words into the wrong ears. Perhaps because they were slaves and he wasn't.

Verax passed the wine on, and rubbed the soft nose of the nearest horse. He was wondering how much longer it would take for Titus to get so obnoxiously drunk that he was asked to leave when there was the sound of footsteps. To his delight a familiar voice slurred, "I'm sure I left a carriage here somewhere."

Verax stepped forward. "Over here, sir!"

The slight figure that reeled into the torchlight wearing a garland tipped over one ear was indeed Titus. But what was Verax supposed to do about the half-naked girl who was clambering into the carriage behind him?

"You need to get down, miss." When she took no notice, he grabbed one braceleted arm. "Miss—"

"Who are you?" The black make-up against the pallor of her face made her eyes look enormous. "Titus? Make him go away!"

"Sir, I have to take you—

"Get away, you fool!"

Something—he guessed later it must have been the young master's foot—hit him in the chest and sent him sprawling back across the paving. Grazed, winded and stunned, Verax was vaguely aware of the carriage door slamming shut above him.

Someone said, "He'll learn." It was a moment before Verax realized the slaves were talking about him, and not about Titus, whose habits they probably knew only too well.

"It's all right," someone else assured him as he picked himself up and rubbed his bruised backside. "Xanthe's a regular."

Indeed, to judge from the sounds that were clearly audible across the courtyard, Xanthe was not only a regular but a professional. She and Titus were holding their own private party inside his father's second-best carriage.

Verax leaned back against a pillar, folded his arms, and tried to imagine he was somewhere else. When the carriage door finally creaked open, he did not bother to offer a helping hand. To his disappointment, neither the girl nor her shambling client fell down the step. Xanthe turned and blew Verax a kiss before linking one slender arm through Titus's, and guiding him back around the rose beds.

When she opened the door Verax heard shouting and a gust of drunken laughter from somewhere deeper inside the house. He yawned, slumped down against the wall where he was safely hidden by the carriage, and closed his eyes.

He must have drifted off to sleep. There were running feet, and men yelling and whooping, and girls shrieking, "Faster, faster!" and somebody shouting "Stop!" and he had no idea what was going on. He leaned sideways to peer around the back of the carriage. In the uncertain torchlight he saw party guests cavorting around the flower beds with girls clinging to their backs and kicking them on like cavalry riders. Somebody was running around waving something above his head. Verax caught a brief glint of silver just as the figure stumbled and swore. Something hit the paving with a metallic clang.

A voice yelled, "You idiot!"

The "horses" raced through the gap between the carriage and the wall. "Mind the animals!" cried Verax, ducking between the humans to hold the real horses as they tossed their heads and stamped in alarm. "Whoa now," he murmured into the nearest whiskery ear. "Steady. Just a few daft lads having some fun."

Across the courtyard someone was yelling, "Not that way! Mind the—oh, for pity's sake!"

"Look out!"

"Oh, shit!"

Verax glanced across in time to see Bacchus crash onto the paving. The tinkling sound that followed suggested that parts of the god of wine had broken off. The harness jingled as the animals shied.

"You clumsy arse!"

"Sorry!"

"That's it! Out! Get out of my house, the lot of you! Piss off home!"

At last, Verax's prayers were answered. The party was over. He carried on murmuring to the horses as a flailing white figure was hauled past them: a young master who had been deftly grabbed by his slave and wrapped in his toga as if he were a dangerous beast. Other staggering youths were being urged towards the open gate with assurances that their fathers would be worrying about them. There was no sign of Titus, but Verax dared not let go of the horses to go and look for him.

The swaddled guest who was stumbling out into the street had managed to get an arm free. He raised one hand as if he were making a speech, announced, "It's all right, everybody! I'll get Pa to pay for it!" and fell over.

That much remained clear in Verax's memory. But he did not recall the sound of the gate being closed, nor the host going back into the house. Later he reasoned that he must have gone to light the carriage torch and then put it in the bracket. He could remember the yellow light spilling onto a pair of feet sticking out of the carriage door. He could remember thinking, *ah, there he is*, and climbing inside to rearrange his drunken master so they could go home.

And then there was someone screaming, very close by. Because the white shape sprawled awkwardly at his feet was indeed Titus, and there was a dark patch beside Titus's head that shouldn't be there, and the kitchen girl was backing away from the door and crying, "He's killed him!"

"Not me!" he gasped, feeling panic rising in his chest. "It wasn't me!"

But the heavy wine jug was in his own right hand and, on the base of the jug, there was blood.

2

Gaius Petreius Ruso's eldest sister reached him first as he helped to haul the baggage in through the gateway. She wasted no time on sentimental greetings. "There you are, Gaius!" was swiftly followed by, "Did you find a job for my husband?"

"You're looking well, Marcia."

"I am, aren't I? So, did you?" When he did not reply she said, "Did you even ask anybody, Gaius?"

Ruso was too hot and grimy from the journey to want a quarrel. "Rome is a marvellous place," he told her. "I'd thoroughly recommend it for a holiday. But—"

"Some of us can't afford holidays!"

He glanced around the sunlit garden. Four years had passed since his last trip home to Gaul, but the fountain basin was still cracked and now the vine-clad pergola was leaning towards it as if trying to see where the water had gone.

Over in the farmyard he heard a shout of, "Master Gaius is here!" From the house came the crash of shutters being flung open, the thunder of footsteps on floorboards and scattered cries of, "Uncle Gaius!" and "They're here!" and "It's Uncle Gaius and that Tilla!"

"Believe me," Ruso told Marcia, "you're better off staying here."

She folded her arms. "Well you would say that,

wouldn't you?"

He was saved from having to reply by a cry of, "Oh, thank the gods!" from his stepmother. She was hurrying down the steps from the house with one arm clutching her stole and the other outstretched as if to seize him before he could escape. He was surprised to see tears of joy in her eyes.

Children and adults were now converging from all directions upon the small party of new arrivals. Ruso caught himself staring at a young woman who must be one of the family, but surely his oldest niece couldn't be that shape yet? Whoever it was looked very much like his sister Flora had looked on his last visit, but Flora must have changed by now. As the pack closed in, he tried desperately to work out which of his younger relatives was which.

"Uncle Gaiuth! Remember me?"

"Of course!" The nephew who had fallen off a fence and knocked his front teeth out. Someone had mentioned the accident in a letter. "How are you?"

"Marthia thed you never bother with family any more but I knew you would come!"

Ruso shot a glance at his wife—Tilla was good at names—but she was already showing off the baby to one of the nieces. Beyond her, their two slaves stood amid the pile of luggage, waiting to be told what to do.

"Oh, Gaius!" His stepmother flung both arms around him, weeping. "Here you are at last! You'll do something, won't you?"

Ruso, who knew better than to agree to anything suggested by Arria without knowing the details, kissed her damp cheek and told her she hadn't changed a bit. She pushed him away, wiping her tears on her stole.

"You'll need to wash before you go, dear. You smell like a farm hand. But do please be quick."

A scatter of slaves had gathered just beyond the main circle: a couple of women drying wet hands on their skirts, the family nursemaid with somebody's baby, the stable boy, and a knot of farm hands grubby from working in the fields. Ruso searched in vain for any sign of his brother or his sister-in-law.

The babble died away. The assembled household seemed to be waiting for some sort of speech. Ruso stepped back, surveyed his audience, and announced, "Thanks, everybody. It's good to be home," just as his own small daughter gave a wail of distress that sent several of the womenfolk hurrying across to offer sympathy and advice. To his stepmother, who was showing no interest in the British baby he had adopted, he said, "We've been on the road since dawn: everyone's tired. Where should we take the luggage?"

"Oh, the staff will see to all that, Gaius! What about poor Flora?"

He glanced around again. None of the crowd could plausibly be his youngest sister. "What about Flora?"

"You will help, won't you, dear? My husband is away and your brother's just gone off and left us. What sort of man takes his wife away to a friend's wedding and leaves his children behind?"

A man seizing the chance for a rare holiday, Ruso supposed.

"My husband can't help either, because he's at work," put in Marcia. "Although for what he gets paid, it's hardly worth the bother. And I can't go, can I? I've got a family to look after now too." She pointed to the infant watching them from the arms of the nursemaid. "You're not the only one with a baby, Gaius. You might think of saying congratulations."

"Congratulations," he told her. "Where's Flora?"

His stepmother's "I don't know!" was more of a howl than a statement. "We thought she was in her room, but she isn't there. The staff have been looking everywhere for her. Nobody's seen her since this morning. Your sister has gone missing!"

Marcia rolled her eyes. "She's not missing, Mother. She's just not here."

Ruso said, "So where is she?"

"It's obvious."

"Why is it obvious?" cried her mother. "Your sister could have been stolen by slave traders and you don't seem the least bit worried!"

"It's obvious," Marcia repeated. "Flora's gone to try and rescue her stupid boyfriend."

"Oh, no!" wailed Arria. "All the way to that awful man's estate, and she hasn't even taken her hat!"

"Flora's boyfriend owns an estate?" Ruso was more surprised by the boyfriend's wealth than by his apparent awfulness.

"No, silly, that's where he works," Marcia explained. "For that hideous old lecher—what's his name?"

"Sabinus," supplied her mother.

"Sabinus," agreed Marcia. "The one who used to come and visit Pa and leer at me instead."

3

Less than half an hour before, Ruso's small party had heaved themselves and their luggage down from amongst a load of cloth bales being carried from the river port at Arelate to Nemausus. It struck him that if he had stayed with the cart, he might have passed Flora on the road. She must have gone on foot, because he could see their own farm vehicle standing unattended while the mules munched on the weeds growing out of the ditch. Had his sister planned to walk the couple of miles to Sabinus's estate? What if some stranger had stopped to offer her a lift?

What if she had accepted?

What if she had arrived safely, unchaperoned, and been welcomed into the presence of the hideous old lecher?

All these things were clearly going through his stepmother's mind too. Along with the worry that even if the hatless Flora survived the trip intact, she would look like a lobster and would have a face as brown as a field slave for the rest of the summer. Arria had just voiced this added cause for alarm when she spotted a vehicle passing along the road from the direction of the senator's estate. To Ruso's relief she hurried away to find a slave who could run fast enough to intercept it and interrogate the driver.

"I don't know what all the fuss is about," Marcia observed. "One of the neighbours is bound to bring her back. I bet they won't let her in over there. It's not as if her boyfriend's anybody important. He's only a wheelwright."

Ruso said, "What's she gone to rescue him from?"

"Although I suppose..." Marcia paused to wind one of her curls around a forefinger. "He might be the one who's been killed."

"What?"

"He's Sabinus's son too," she said, as if that explained everything. "At least, that's what he told Flora. But only by a slave woman, so he doesn't really count."

Ruso took a deep breath. "Marcia, what exactly is Flora involved with?"

"We don't know."

"You must have some idea. Someone's been killed?"

The curls bounced in agreement. "Cook went into town this morning to buy some—oh, I can't remember. Something we haven't got."

"Does it matter?"

"Not really," Marcia conceded. "Anyway, the big news at market is that there was trouble at a party last night, and Sabinus's son is dead, and Flora's boyfriend's got something to do with it."

Ruso's hope that a neighbour might deliver his youngest sister home at any moment began to fade. "Flora's boyfriend was in a fight with Sabinus's son?"

"Possibly. You know what gossip is like."

Ruso sighed. "I suppose I'd better get over there."

"Can you take Ma with you? She's driving us all mad."

"No," he told her. "Absolutely not."

Despite Ruso's decision to carry on smelling like a

farm hand, he did not set out immediately. There was a worrying pause between him ordering the mules to move on and their deciding that they liked him enough to obey. In the meantime his wife, sitting beside him on the driver's bench, squeezed his arm and murmured, "Thank you for taking me."

He grunted a response, waiting for some sign of equine co-operation.

"Your family are very..." Tilla's voice tailed off as she sought a suitable word.

"I know," he said, not admitting that he had brought her not only to rescue her but because he was afraid this was serious, and because he knew too that his stepmother would be less keen to come if Tilla was there.

"At last!" he said, and the cart jolted forward.

4

Flora was nowhere on the paved main road, nor on the dusty drive that led through Sabinus's extensive vineyards and olive groves. Ahead, set up on a slope to catch the breeze, one of the most expensive villas in the district basked in the afternoon sun—but before she could reach it, Flora would have had to get past the heavy wooden gates in the boundary wall.

Ruso jumped down from the cart and saw movement behind the iron grille set in the right-hand gate. "Gaius Petreius Ruso," he told it. He had barely begun to explain his visit when there was a squeal of hinges and the gate swung back to reveal an arched passageway with a door set into one side and another set of gates at the far end.

"You'll be come for the young lady, sir." The hulking gatekeeper sounded as relieved to get rid of Flora as Ruso was to find her. "She's right here."

"Gaius?" called a female voice from behind the door. "Is that you?"

"Flora?"

"They won't let me in!"

"It's all right, Flora. I've come to get you."

"Tell them I'm not leaving until they let him go."

"But I've—"

"It wasn't his fault!"

The big man shuffled awkwardly. "I couldn't let the

young lady go no further, sir," he said. "To be honest, if anybody catches her where she is I'm in trouble."

"Of course you couldn't," Ruso agreed. "Especially today. I hear you've had a bereavement."

The man nodded. "Young Master Titus, sir. A terrible loss to us all."

So Marcia had been right first time: the heir was dead.

"I shouldn't have let her in there at all, sir, only she was a bit hot and bothered, and with her being a neighbour..."

"I'll take her home," Ruso promised, wondering if he could persuade Flora to apologize. From the other side of the gatehouse door he heard, "I'm not moving from this bench until they do something!" and dismissed the idea as hopeless.

He felt his wife's hand on his arm. "I will go," she murmured. "You will only argue with her."

Moments later both men were shut out and Ruso heard, "Flora! What is all this about poor Verax?"

Verax? Was that the name of the boyfriend? How did women know these things?

"She'll be out in a moment," he promised.

"Yes, sir." The gatekeeper stepped to one side.

Ruso folded his arms and leaned back against the cool of the shaded wall. "She won't be long."

"No, sir."

Out in the sunshine, the cicadas trilled and the bees buzzed and the metal fastenings on the harness jingled as one of the mules tossed its head and stamped. He said, "If anyone comes, I'll explain that you were helping a neighbour."

"Thank you, sir."

Ruso wondered if he should move the animals out of the sun. "I don't want to intrude," he said, "but I've only just arrived back in the province. What happened to your young master?"

"He suffered a blow to the head, sir. While visiting a friend in town."

"And this Verax was there too?"

"He was, sir."

"Is it true there was a fight?"

The gatekeeper shifted his stance. "Perhaps you'd better wait outside, sir."

The big gate screeched back into place, leaving the gatekeeper now harbouring not one but two uninvited females on his master's property.

Ruso persuaded the mules forward, taking the cart around in as tight a circle as it could perform. Watching the outer wheel roll perilously close to the ditch at the edge of the track, he wondered why Titus had taken his father's wheelwright with him on last night's fatal trip to town. It was hard to imagine, even if there really had been a fight, that it had taken place between the two of them. More likely Verax was now being punished for failing to protect Titus from somebody else. Doubtless when things settled down he would be released. In the meantime Flora's antics could only make things worse for him.

He stationed the mules in the shade of the trees. They stood swishing their tails against the flies while he drank some of the water he had brought for his sister. He wondered what Tilla was saying to her, and why Flora could not see how inappropriate it was to foist herself on a newly-bereaved household. He stashed the water skin back under the logs that nobody had had time to unload.

As he gazed out over the tall ears of the mules, it struck him that despite the coating of road dust, these animals were far more polished than farm transport required. That would be the work of the stable boy, who probably still hadn't forgiven the family for selling the horses. The family debt was such that the stable boy was lucky they hadn't sold him too, but Ruso supposed he was unlikely to see it that way.

A couple of messengers from town came and went, churning up more dust.

Ruso decided Flora didn't deserve the water and finished it himself.

He had just resolved to go in and haul his sister out when he heard the screech of hinges and his wife reappeared. "You will never believe what has happened!" Tilla exclaimed. "I told Flora, she must tell you all about it."

"Hello, Flora," Ruso said, seizing the hand of the tousled young woman who had once been his little sister and hauling her up onto the bench beside him. "What's happened?"

"Gaius. Hello." Flora paused to tug her skirts straight before settling on the bench. "You heard what's happened to Titus?"

"Yes."

"Well obviously it's terrible, but I promise you it's not Verax's fault."

"Isn't it?"

"Of course not. If you knew him like I do you wouldn't even ask."

"I see."

"He's not what you think, Gaius!"

"You don't know what I think."

From her position behind them in the cart, his wife reached up and jabbed a finger into his side, which struck him as deeply disloyal.

"I can tell from your face that you disapprove," Flora insisted. "And you haven't even met him."

"I don't disapprove," he told her, gathering up the reins. "I don't know him. This is my reserving judgement face."

She shifted beside him. "This is serious, Gaius! He could be—oh, I can't bear to think about it!"

"Flora, we've travelled over a thousand miles and I'm tired. I can't help my face. Get on with it."

"Did you bring any water?"

The cart jolted forwards. "No."

"Verax would never do anything to hurt Titus. I know because he told me. So whoever's killed him, it isn't Verax. They're brothers, for goodness' sake! Everybody knows about Verax being Sabinus's son too. And now that mean old man on the gate says they've got him chained up in the slave quarters and he won't even go and tell him I'm here. I don't know why they're being so horrible to him. He works really hard and he's always doing people favours and everyone likes him."

There were certainly some people who didn't like him now, but Ruso was saved from replying by a shout of, "Sir!" He twisted round on the bench to see the gatekeeper hurrying towards them down the drive.

"Sir, the master wants a word—just you, sir," the man added as Flora made to climb down.

"Tell him you want to see Verax," Flora urged him. "Tell Verax I was here and not to worry, it will all be all right."

Ruso jumped to the ground. "I'll walk home."

Tilla, grasping the need to get Flora away before she changed her mind about leaving, scrambled forward to where he had been sitting. As she gathered up the reins he heard Flora say, "You are going to drive us?"

Tilla said, "Why not?"

Flora paused. Then she said, "Yes! Why not?"

The wheels rumbled away down the drive. Ruso made an effort to straighten the tunic he'd been travelling in since early morning, and ran his hands through his hair. To judge from the expression on the face of the old man in the gateway who was watching his approach, his efforts to improve his appearance hadn't had a great deal of effect.

5

The figure with thin hair and sagging features who was easing his way forward with the help of a walking stick was indeed Sabinus, but the heavy brows had faded to grey. The jaw that had once looked strong now looked gaunt above the dark toga of a man in mourning.

"You're the other Petreius boy."

The voice was hoarser than he remembered. "Ruso, sir."

Had Sabinus been a hideous old lecher? Ruso hadn't been aware of it. But then neither had he been aware that Sabinus and several other friends were lending his father ridiculous sums of money that he wouldn't be able to pay back. Now, Ruso's father was long dead—although the debts weren't—and Sabinus was only an echo of the man Ruso could still picture roaring with laughter at some joke in his father's study.

Ruso said, "I was very sorry to hear about Titus, sir."

The nod was brief, as if he was tired of sympathy. "That sister of yours. You need to get her under control."

"My wife's taking her home now, sir. I'm sorry if she caused a disturbance."

There was no reply.

"With your permission, sir, I'd like to pay my respects to your son. I'll go home first and change out of travelling clothes."

The old man glanced at Ruso's creased and sweat-stained tunic. Its original colour had been lost in the wash long ago, and even when clean it would not have been suitable for mourning. Despite this, Sabinus gave a jerk of the head that indicated Ruso was to follow. "If the girl comes back," he told the gatekeeper, "get one of our people to take her straight home."

Another slave in a dark tunic was waiting inside the gates. He appeared to be a secretary, who fell into step behind Sabinus so that the three of them formed a slow procession through the working yard of the estate. The sounds of hammering and sawing faded into silence at their approach. Slaves in ordinary clothes stopped to bow to their frail master as he passed through all the accumulated wealth he must surely have been planning to hand on to his son: workshops and wood stores and vegetable plots, pottering chickens and loaded donkeys, a high-windowed building that might have been a bunkhouse, and a stable block where horses gazed out at them over wooden half-doors. At the end of the block was a large covered area where a farm cart had been dismantled and abandoned in mid-repair. Ruso guessed this was—or had been—Verax's workshop. Beyond it a slave stepped down from the open doorway of a smart four-wheeled carriage. He tucked a cleaning rag behind his back while he bowed.

Sabinus stared at the carriage. "I want that got rid of."

"I'll see to it, sir," the secretary promised. "Would you like a replacement vehicle?"

Sabinus grunted. "What's the point?"

Another wall lay ahead of them. The fresh limewash was a dazzling white in the sunshine but the roses clambering over the gateway had been half-obscured by gloomy branches of cypress. Ruso followed Sabinus through to a garden filled with the scent of lavender. A tree-lined path offered a shady route to the house he had glimpsed from the road.

More cypress hung over the colonnaded walkway that ran the length of the building. As they passed beneath it Ruso's vision took a few moments to adjust from the bright sun, but the heavy smell of incense and roses and something else less desirable would have told him this was Titus's resting-place, even if there had not been torches burning at the head and foot of the bier.

The sound of weeping mingled with the slow notes of a pipe drifting across from the far corner. Ruso became aware of servants standing against the walls, keeping watch over their master.

"They said I should hire mourners," said Sabinus. "I told them, *I won't have my boy surrounded by wailing strangers. He's suffered enough already.*"

Ruso bowed his head, gave a nod to the shrine of the household gods, and approached the bier. The figure that lay on it was swathed in a pure white toga. Below the crowning garland of flowers, the delicate features of the dead youth bore little resemblance to Sabinus either now or in his prime.

One of the staff stepped forward and indicated a smoking burner and a bowl of incense. Ruso was dropping a few more golden grains onto the burner when soft footsteps approached from the house and a slave whispered to the secretary, who in turn informed Sabinus that "Germanicus Publius is here, sir."

"Eh?"

"The young man from the house, sir. Last night's host."

Ruso already knew who Germanicus Publius was. He was the son of another "friend" who had lent his father money. Surprised that Publius Senior had not come to support his son on this awkward visit, he made a mental note to go and pay his respects to the old man first thing in the morning. Meanwhile Sabinus raised a hand to scratch his head, releasing a shower of the ash he must have flung there as a token of grief. "I suppose we have to let him in."

Moments later a youth entered and bowed, first to the bier and then to Sabinus. Ruso stepped back, recognising the former boy in the tall, well-built youth whose early promise of good looks had been fulfilled. Publius Junior, visibly sweating inside a toga that might once have been black, took no notice of him, perhaps mistaking him for a farm slave. It was an understandable error. Even Publius's slave, a small man cursed with a squint so dreadful that Ruso recognized him instantly, was better dressed than Ruso.

Publius said, "Please accept the condolences of all my household, sir."

Sabinus thanked him without looking at him.

From his position in the background Ruso could see that while the young man's left hand was occupied with holding his toga together in the appropriate manner, the right fist was tightly clenched behind his back.

"I'm distraught that such a dreadful thing should have happened in my house."

If Publius had been hoping for reassurance that he was in no way to blame, Sabinus's silence must have been disappointing.

"And so soon after the loss of my own father."

So that was why Publius Senior wasn't here. Ruso felt

sadder than he would have expected at the news that another of the old guard had gone. And faintly ashamed at the thought that if he went to offer his condolences to Publius Senior's family tomorrow, he would be able to examine the scene of the fatal party.

One of Sabinus's staff glided forward and indicated the incense burner, just as he had to Ruso. Publius dropped in a couple more grains and the smoke seemed to catch in his throat. He took a hasty step backwards. For a few moments the music of the pipes was drowned by the sound of coughing.

When Publius could breathe again he said, "I'm having all my staff thoroughly questioned, sir. Just to make absolutely sure of what happened."

He was clearly attempting to do the right thing, which was bad news for his slaves. They would not be able to pretend that they hadn't been there: the usual desperate claim of frightened staff now the emperor had ruled that only slaves who were likely to know something about a case should be tortured for evidence.

"I'll let you know if I find out anything of interest, sir."

Somewhere over in the yard, a man was shouting. Alarm or anger: it was hard to tell. Sabinus gazed at his dead son. "Will the questions bring Titus back?"

Publius was clenching his fist behind his back again. "May I ask, sir—what's to happen to the driver?"

"Young Verax should never have been driving in the first place." Sabinus reached forward to shoo a fly from his son's cheek, and sighed. "But, once a dog has bitten, it has to be destroyed."

Ruso swallowed. He had hoped Sabinus might show his illegitimate son some mercy.

Publius said, "Maybe one of my staff will—"

"I thank the gods neither of their mothers is around to see this."

"I don't think our kitchen maid actually saw the blow being struck, sir."

Sabinus did not reply, and Publius had the sense to let the music fill the silence. No words could offer comfort for the terrible betrayal Sabinus had suffered: one son killing the other.

The pause was interrupted by more shouting from beyond the garden wall. A farm slave was racing down the main path towards the house.

Publius began to gather up the folds of his toga. "I can see you're busy, sir," he said. "I'll let you know if my staff have anything useful to say. Perhaps one of them can help to explain what happened."

But Sabinus wasn't listening. Ruso heard the secretary murmur, "The master really isn't himself at the moment, sir," as he ushered Publius and his man back into the house and presumably away through another exit.

One of the waiting staff detached himself from the wall and hurried down the steps to meet the breathless man in the garden, then came back and whispered something to Sabinus, whose head jerked up. "Are you sure?"

More whispering.

"Well he can't have got far." Sabinus raised a hand, and the music fell silent. "We need to carry out a search."

"Everyone!" announced the secretary, beckoning to the staff stationed around the walls. The musician joined the other slaves in hurrying towards him. A couple of them glanced at the body and then at their master, but

Ruso assured Sabinus he would stay with the bier, and they left to join the group already being given orders down in the garden.

After a hasty conversation three slaves trotted back to the house and disappeared through various doors. The others headed for the farmyard with Sabinus shooing them ahead and limping in their wake.

Ruso wandered across to the wooden railing that overlooked the garden. His heart began to beat faster as Sabinus disappeared through the archway to the yard. He should not do what he was about to do, but there would never be another chance like this. Tilla would have told him it was a gift from the gods.

A swift glance around told him the entrance hall was empty. Wishing he had his own toga to hide behind, he strolled across to the bier and stationed himself with his back to the garden, facing one of the doors through which someone might emerge at any moment.

This was disrespectful.

This was necessary.

He shifted the finely-woven wool of Titus's toga with one forefinger. The visible surfaces of the lad's slender hands and wrists were unmarked. There was no sign that he had made any effort to defend himself.

A blow to the head, the doorkeeper had said.

There was no obvious damage to the face or the crown of the head. Ruso glanced up to make sure the house door was still shut, then gently raised the wreath of roses three or four inches with both hands, afraid it might spring apart in his fingers.

There was nothing to see.

From inside the house he could hear running footsteps, the calling-out of orders, doors banging and the scrape of furniture being shifted.

Ruso leaned forward, murmured, "Forgive me," and slid a hand behind the wreath and under the head of young Titus.

"Gaius Petreius!"

Ruso spun round, his heart racing. How had Sabinus reached the foot of the garden steps without making a sound? How long had he been standing there? Long enough to see Ruso repositioning the wreath? Long enough, even, to see him palpating the depressed fracture at the back of Titus's skull?

He tried to get his breathing under control. "Sir?"

"Did you have something to do with this?"

As his mind fumbled for an explanation of why he had been touching the corpse, Ruso became aware that Sabinus was asking the wrong question. "Sir?"

Sabinus scowled. "At least have the decency not to treat me like a fool. Verax. He isn't where we left him. He's escaped."

"Sir?"

Sabinus sighed. "You and that sister of yours. Is that what you were up to?"

"Not at all, sir," Ruso assured him, realizing with a rush of relief that he had got away with it. He added truthfully, "I know nothing about it," and then with less conviction, "Nor does my sister."

"You'd better not be lying to me."

In other circumstances Ruso might have cared that Sabinus didn't trust him. As things stood, he was delighted to be accused of the wrong thing. "I have no idea where he is, sir. Or where he was." With luck, Flora's unlucky choice of boyfriend had run away and would never be seen again.

"Hmph." Sabinus began to work his way up, pausing on each step to bring the second foot to join the first before setting off again.

"Sir, is it possible Verax is innocent?"

But Sabinus did not seem to be listening. "Should have sent him away years ago," he said. "Too soft with him. Made the mistake of listening to his mother." He raised the stick, a thin stripe against the blue sky. It swung down and hit the wooden railing with a crack. "Women! They're a weakness."

"Sir—"

"I never dreamed it would come to this. Both my boys! The gods have had their revenge."

"Sir, Verax may not—"

"Don't torment me!"

"Sir, let me make some enquiries. It can't make things any worse. I can say I'm doing it for my sister."

Sabinus shrugged. "Do what you like. I want nothing to do with it." He eased his way across to the bier and gazed down at his lost son. "I've got a funeral to arrange."

6

Tilla waited until she and Flora were well clear of the estate and jolting along the main road before asking, "Who would want to hurt this Titus?"

Flora shrugged. "Who wouldn't? I couldn't tell you back at his house, but everybody hates him. He's a creep."

"A creep?"

"When people first meet him—I mean, met him—they thought he was really friendly," she said. "But he wasn't like that underneath. He was always bragging to his friends about the rich girls he'd done it with. And he thought it was funny to play tricks on people. Like when my friend was up in the high seats watching the gladiators, and he sneaked up behind her and put a live mouse down the back of her dress."

Tilla shuddered, imagining the horror of something furry scurrying around inside her clothing.

"She jumped up and fell onto the people in the next row down and some old lady got hurt and there was lots of trouble and they all got thrown out. Titus told everyone it was her own fault for making such a fuss."

"That is bad," Tilla agreed, reining back the mules as the ox wagon in front slowed to a crawl on the long incline.

"Then once they were all out drinking and Titus

waited till the serving-man went to the latrine and he put a scorpion under a cup on the bar."

Tilla was too busy sizing up the speed of the carriage approaching in the distance to reply.

"And then they all laughed when the man got stung."

She urged the mules into a trot and steered them out past the lumbering cart.

Flora said, "Are you not afraid the beasts will run away?"

"No," Tilla assured her, hoping they were as well trained as they seemed to be, and squinting at the approaching carriage.

She could see the flying manes of the horses galloping towards her. Her own vehicle was still parallel with the cart. Flora was still talking. The approaching driver was frantically hauling on the reins. Tilla could see his mouth moving. She cried out to urge the mules on, and just managed to bring them back in before the carriage thundered past, its wheels missing their own by inches. Whatever the driver yelled at them was lost in the noise, as was Flora's retort of, "You should learn to drive!" and then when the carriage was gone, "Stupid man! Does he think he's at the races?"

Tilla, suspecting the near miss had been her own fault, wiped the perspiration off her forehead and decided she liked her sister-in-law more than she had realized.

"Anyway," Flora continued, "Titus."

"Titus," said Tilla, speaking more kind words to the animals and glad her husband's family drove mules and not horses, which would have been much harder to settle after the excitement.

"Everyone says he's worse since he went to Rome,"

said Flora. "I don't know why Marcia wants to go to Rome if they're all like that. Thinking they're so superior and they know everything and out here in the provinces we're practically barbarians—oh, sorry."

"That must be very annoying," Tilla told her, ignoring the insult to her British ancestors.

"Verax heard he got sent home early because he got into trouble all the time. All the estate staff were praying for the day he went off to join the Legions. I expect his real driver was just pretending to be ill so he didn't have to put up with him."

"Somebody liked him enough to invite him to a party," Tilla pointed out.

"I told you, he could be nice when he wanted something. Or when he had to talk his way out of trouble."

"He sounds very annoying," Tilla agreed. "But was he so bad that people would want to kill him?"

"He was horrible."

Something about her tone prompted Tilla to ask, "Did he do something to you?"

The cart had trundled on for a good few paces before Flora said, "It wasn't anything much. It's got nothing to do with what happened to him."

"Tell me."

"It was nothing," Flora insisted. "I told you, he was like that with everybody."

"Like what?"

Another pause. "Promise me you won't tell my brother."

Tilla shook her head. "He must know everything if he is to help. But you don't have to tell him yourself if you don't want to. I will do it."

Flora was silent as they passed a crossroads where a little shrine was decked with wilting flowers. Finally she said, "It was when I went with my other brother to deliver something to the estate. Verax was busy working and Lucius went off to talk to the steward, and Titus got me in a room on my own."

"Oh, Flora!" Tilla glanced at her. "I am sorry."

"Oh, no, it wasn't that bad!" Flora shifted beside her on the bench. "It was just talk. I can't even remember what he said. It was the way he said it. And the way he looked at me. Sort of... so he knew I knew what he meant. It made me go all squirmy inside. I didn't know what to say so I just pretended not to understand. And afterwards I felt really..." She stopped, searching for a word. "Stupid. Angry with myself."

"Did Verax know?"

"I never told Verax he *did* anything. Truly I didn't. And they sorted it out between them at the time."

"How did they sort it out?"

Flora pulled at a crease in her dress. "Verax went to see him," she said. "Titus was all slime and politeness and said he hadn't meant to insult me, and he went on about what a lucky man Verax was."

"And then?"

"And then nothing," said Flora. "That was it. So it's got nothing to do with last night, has it?"

"I don't expect so."

"Of course it hasn't! I wish I hadn't told you now. We need to go right here."

Tilla had already begun to make the turn onto the farm track. In just this short distance, she had learned much about Titus, she had changed her mind about Flora, and she had narrowly avoided a serious accident.

Verax had been obliged to make a much longer journey in the sole company of a spoiled half-brother who had insulted his girl. Whatever had been going through his mind by the time they arrived at the party was not likely to have been friendly.

Ahead, one of the slaves swung open the gate to let them through. There was a shriek of "Flora!" from the house.

At the sight of her mother running towards her with arms wide, Flora gave a dramatic sigh and then cried, "It's all right, Mother, I'm fine!"

The slave was called to help Flora down from the cart while her mother demanded to know whether she was *really* fine. Was she quite sure? "We've all been so worried about you!"

"We just nearly got crashed into by a mad driver," Flora announced. "You should have seen him! Tilla only just got us out of the way in time."

"Did Gaius not go with you?" Arria peered into the cart as if Tilla might have tied him up and thrown him into the back with the logs. "What have you done with my stepson?"

Tilla said, "He stayed behind to talk to someone."

"Gaius is going to see Verax and tell him not to worry and everything will be all right," Flora explained. "Can somebody get me some water? I'm about to die of thirst."

Arria frowned. "But how will it be all right?"

"Because Verax didn't do it, of course," said Flora.

7

The farm hands had finished work for the day and gone in for dinner. Ruso leaned on the study windowsill and thought of the times his father must have stood here while the stillness of the early evening settled on the vineyard. Watching the low sun dappling the leaves and gradually giving way to dusk. Hearing the last trills of the cicadas: the sound Tilla called "that screechy noise". The sound that he always thought of as the music of home. Had this tranquil view given his father peace from his worries? Or had the voices of his creditors whispered to him even here?

From deeper inside the house Ruso heard running footsteps. A door slammed, a child squealed, and another was shouting, "That's mine! Give it back!"

The words of the reply were unintelligible, but the tone was not.

"You're supposed to be in bed!" cried the outraged victim. "If Ma was here—"

Another muffled reply.

"Well when she gets back I'm going to tell her!"

Another door banging, or possibly the same one. Then an adult voice, demanding to know what was going on.

Ruso glanced over his shoulder to check that he had secured the latch. To be part of a large and healthy family was a great blessing, but sometimes that blessing was best appreciated from the privacy of a quiet study. A man with responsibilities needed somewhere to marshal his thoughts and—

He leaned further out of the window, shading his eyes and peering between the gnarled trunks of the vines to where he had seen movement. It was too early in the year to worry about human thieves, but an animal left to wander could cause a lot of damage. A visit from a goat would be a disaster. Should he go to check? On the other hand, venturing out would mean being accosted by the rampaging nephews and nieces.

He squinted out between the spindly rows for a long time, but nothing seemed to be moving now. He turned to the indoor gloom. He needed to concentrate his thoughts on the problem of Flora's boyfriend.

He would have liked to talk the whole thing over with his brother while steaming pleasantly in the farm bathhouse with the door locked, but Lucius wasn't here. The bathhouse might as well not have been here, either. As Marcia had explained over dinner, the bath boy had recently died of old age and Lucius had been too mean to buy a replacement. "So the whole place is useless. If we want to bathe properly we have to go into town."

"It's not useless, dear," her mother had intervened. "The other staff light the furnace for special occasions."

"But we never have any special occasions."

"Never mind," Ruso told them, noting that his own arrival wasn't deemed special enough to celebrate. "It's too hot anyway."

His remark had been followed by a sudden clatter from across the dining room. Something—a chunk of bread?—skittered across the mosaic and vanished under a cupboard. “Why does it matter?” cried Flora, scrambling to her feet. “Poor Verax is all alone and he’s going to be tortured and killed and I’ll die an old maid and you’re all here discussing stupid bathhouses!”

“But Flora dear, we can’t—”

“And Gaius didn’t even talk to him when I asked him to!”

“Please, dear—”

“You all pretend you care but you don’t!” With that, Flora ran out of the room in tears and Tilla abandoned the meal to follow her.

Ruso had seen neither of them since. He could have told Flora that Verax probably wasn’t being tortured, but for the moment he wanted to keep the escape a secret. This business was messy enough already.

He hauled his father’s chair up to the desk. In a moment he would need to call for a light.

The door rattled as someone tried to enter, but the latch held. “It’s me!” announced Marcia. After a moment there was a dull thud as if she had kicked the door. “I know you’re in there, Gaius.”

“What do you want?”

“I’m your sister. Do I have to want something?”

When he released the latch she put her head around the door and said, “You don’t have to sit here in the dark, you know. Even Lucius lets us light the lamps once in a while.”

It was an uncomfortable reminder of his brother’s struggles to pay off the family debt. He said, “Where is this wedding they’ve gone to, exactly?”

“No idea,” Marcia admitted. “But they said they’ll be away for several days and they only went yesterday.”

It was bad news, in more ways than one. Wherever

Lucius went, the key to the ornately carved, iron-bound chest in the corner went too. With it went any chance of getting at the documents that would tell Ruso how much the family had owed to young Publius's late father—and presumably now owed to young Publius. Ruso could hardly go and visit, even to offer condolences, without some sort of grip on his own affairs. He glanced in the direction of the chest and wondered if he should fetch a crow-bar.

"Actually," Marcia said, "I'm here to do you a favour. I'm bringing advance warning that Mother's planning to accost you about expansion plans for the west wing."

"What on earth for, if we can't even afford a bath slave?"

"I'm guessing," said Marcia, flinging herself on the couch, "that since you've just been on holiday in Rome, she thinks you've got some money."

"I haven't been on holiday!"

"That's not what you said before. You said Rome is a very good place for a—"

"Yes, but—"

"And you've bought yourself two slaves."

"Well whatever I had," he told her, "I've spent it. And I don't know how much there is here, because Lucius is away and I can't get into the money chest."

Marcia was on her feet again. "I'll fetch a light. Don't lock me out, because if you do, you'll regret it."

He had barely closed the shutters to keep the moths out when she was back, dark curls casting shadows over her face from the glow of lamplight. This time she secured the latch behind her. "I'll tell you where the spare key to the chest is," she announced, "if you tell me what's going on with Flora's boyfriend."

Spare key? Why had no-one ever told him about this? Now he was going to have to negotiate for it, because any appeal to Marcia's better nature would be a waste of time. "As I said at dinner," he told her, "they didn't let me see him."

"They could have told you to go away at the gate. What did they let you in for?"

"To pay my respects to Titus. Where's this key?"

"You must have found out something. I promise I won't say a word to Flora."

Ruso leaned back in the chair and put his hands behind his head. "How do I know there really is a spare?"

Marcia shrugged. "Suit yourself. I'm not bothered whether you get in there or not."

"I'm the head of the household," he pointed out. "I can insist you give me the key."

"And I can tell Flora you lied to her."

"I didn't."

"But you haven't told me everything. I can tell." She raised the lamp to get a better view of him. "Don't let Mother catch you leaning Pa's chair on the back legs, Gaius. She'll make your life a misery."

Ruso fought down a childish urge to lean even further. "Tell me. What do you think of Verax?"

Marcia pondered this question for a moment. "Boring," she said. "He's quite good looking, but... Well, when we went to the races, all the normal people were cheering on the horses and shouting for the drivers, but Verax—he didn't say a word. So we asked him what was the matter and he said nothing was the matter, he was just busy watching."

Ruso scratched one ear with his forefinger. "That's not what I meant."

"You mean do I think he'd kill somebody? I shouldn't think so, not unless he bored them to death. But he's quite well-built with all that sawing and hammering, so I suppose he wouldn't find it hard."

"And Titus was his half-brother."

"So they say. I can't see him murdering Titus out of jealousy, though. I mean he's not going to get invited to dinner parties or inherit the estate just because Titus is dead, is he? So, do you want this key or not?"

Ruso paused. "How well do you know Publius Germanicus?"

Marcia pursed her lips while she pondered this change of direction. "I know his sister."

"That might be useful. I need to talk to them. The party where Titus died was at their house."

"Hah! I might have guessed."

He waited to be enlightened.

"Publius and his sister have been squabbling ever since their pa died. They had another huge argument the other day. He says she fell down the stairs, but everyone knows he pushed her. Anyway, she's gone off to the country house to get away from him. I suppose he thinks he can have parties every night now."

"What can you tell me about the parties?"

She raised her eyebrows. "Nothing. I'm a respectable married woman."

He held out his hand, palm up. "Key."

Marcia leaned down sideways from the couch. "Lift this corner of the desk, will you?"

He obliged, and when she reappeared there was an object wrapped in grubby linen in her hand. "It sits under the leg and stops the desk from wobbling," she explained, picking apart a knot in the linen and letting it unravel. A key clattered onto the desk. “I found it ages ago. I knew it would—” She stopped. “Verax *is* still alive, isn’t he?”

“I believe so.”

“What does that mean?”

“It means,” he told her, “he was spoken of as if he was alive.”

“What did they say?”

“I’m not telling you.”

“I gave you the key!”

“And I told you where the party was.”

She said, “I’ll tell Mother you’ve got it, so you’re ready to talk money with her.”

He shrugged. “Go ahead. I’m not as frightened of her as you seem to be.”

“Did you really ask to see Verax when you went in there? Or did you just make polite conversation?”

He got to his feet. “That’s it, Marcia. If you can think of anything that’ll help, let me know.”

She grinned. “Fair enough. Mother isn’t really coming, by the way. She and Lucius don’t argue about money any more. Not since she married that dopey builder. Lucius just says yes to everything and then she asks Dopey to do it and he says he’ll put it on his list, and it never costs a thing because he never gets around to it.”

It was Ruso’s turn to smile. Because Lucius was coping with their stepmother better than he’d thought, and because Marcia was as sharp as ever, but mostly because she had just helped him to get access to the information he wanted without being told what it was.

The smile did not last long after she had gone. It faded as soon as he found the right account and saw exactly how much money the young party host could decide to call in from them if things got awkward.

8

The dog had not barked for long, but the sound had been enough to raise the alarm. Ruso lifted his head from Flora's pillow and waited, trying to make out the shape of the room in the darkness. Before long, as he expected, there was a soft tap on the door. Then the tapping turned into a gentle scratching and a whisper of, "Flora?"

Ruso rolled out of bed, taking the blanket with him. He felt his way to the door, lifted the latch and stepped aside.

He was prepared for the violence of a desperate man. What he wasn't prepared for was the clumsy embrace of muscular arms, hot breath on his cheek and a brief scrape of stubble against his own before the visitor cried out in alarm and sprang back.

Ruso flung the blanket. The visitor dodged. Ruso grabbed at him. He missed, but the visitor gave a sudden lurch sideways, swore and crashed to the floor. Ruso threw himself on top and they both rolled across the bedroom tangled in the blanket.

Finally they came to a halt against the wall, both breathing heavily. The blanket was wound around them, forcing an unwanted intimacy with Ruso on top. He still had no idea what Flora's boyfriend looked like, but it was clear that Marcia was right: years of working with wood and iron had given him the sort of physique that could kill an enemy with one blow.

The visitor growled, “I don’t want to hurt you.”

“Good,” Ruso told him. “I don’t want to be hurt.”

“Who are you? What have you done with Flora?”

“We need to talk.”

“Let me go.” Verax began to struggle, but as long as Ruso remained where he was, the blanket held them swaddled together. Finally the thrashing about stopped. Verax strained away from him. “Flora!” he yelled. “Flora, where are you? Flo-ra!”

“Shut up!” Ruso struggled to get a hand free to clamp over the man’s mouth. “Do you want to get caught?”

“Let me go!”

“Half the house must be awake by now. If you try and run, they’ll catch you and send you back.” Ruso rolled away from the wall. “Stay where you are and keep quiet.”

He staggered upright just as the inevitable footsteps came padding along the corridor and faint yellow streaks appeared around the door. Anxious voices began asking each other what was going on, and “Did you hear that shouting?” and “Something about Flora?”

Ruso lifted the latch and put his head out. He glanced around at the cook, the kitchen boy, a tousled Marcia on the arm of her young husband, and then the figure of his own wife approaching from the far end of the corridor. He said, “What’s going on?”

“Somebody was shouting,” said Marcia.

“Oh, sorry,” he said. “It was probably me again.”

She peered at him. “What are you doing in Flora’s room, Gaius?”

“I talk in my sleep,” he told her. It keeps the family awake, so I’ve come in here to give them a quiet night. Flora’s over with the cousins.”

"You talk about *Flora* in your sleep?" demanded Marcia, clearly incredulous.

Ruso scratched his head. "So it seems."

More footsteps were approaching, and another lamp. He hoped it wasn't Flora herself, who would point out that she had been evicted from her room on the grounds that he and Tilla needed a rest—together—from their sleepless baby. To his relief it was only his stepmother, her skin glistening with face cream.

"It's all right, Mother," Marcia told her. "It's just Gaius gone mad."

His stepmother, who seemed to find this entirely credible, shuffled away down the corridor.

"He talks at night when he is very tired, or he is anxious about something," put in Tilla. "When it is really bad, he shouts."

"It's true," said Ruso, seizing the lifeline she had thrown him. "We were very worried about Flora this afternoon."

Tilla said, "Your sister is safely home, husband. Go back to sleep."

He glanced around the figures gathered in the corridor: bare feet, rumpled tunics, bedtime hair framing anxious faces. "Sorry I disturbed you all," he said. "I'll try not to do it again."

Marcia said, "How are you going to stop yourself if you're asleep?"

Tilla stepped forward and placed a hand on his arm. "I will stay with him," she said.

"Mad!" muttered Marcia, turning to steer her own husband in the direction of the stairs. "No wonder he couldn't find a job in Rome."

9

Tilla had brought a lamp, so Ruso was at last able to see the uninvited guest now eying them from behind the door. The square jawline reminded him far more of a younger Sabinus than Titus's delicate features had done. "Sit down," he said, indicating the foot of Flora's empty sleeping-couch and settling himself at the head.

Verax remained standing. "You're Flora's other brother? The doctor?"

"I am."

"Can I see her now?"

"No." Ruso retrieved the jumbled blanket from the floor and tucked it around his wife, who had curled up in the wicker chair. Meanwhile the wheelwright shifted from one foot to the other and glanced at the door. "What are you going to do?"

Ruso said, "I've been wondering that ever since I saw you in the vineyard."

Verax sighed. "I knew coming here was a bad idea."

Ruso, who had promised Sabinus he would keep an eye open for the fugitive, said, "It's the first place anyone would look." Fortunately he had avoided promising to do anything about it if he found him.

"I just want to say goodbye to her."

Tilla said, "Flora asked us to help you."

The man glanced at Ruso. "Will you let me see her?"

"Probably not."

"Once I've spoken to her I'll go away and you'll never see me again."

"Nothing would please me more," Ruso admitted. "But unfortunately, that's not what everyone else wants." He leaned back into the corner of the couch. "I went to Sabinus's estate this afternoon and paid my respects to young Titus."

"It wasn't me who killed him, sir." Verax had now recovered his senses enough to show some respect.

"Do you know who did?"

"No, sir. But that doesn't matter, does it? They all think it was me."

"Who do you think did it?" put in Tilla.

The bed creaked as the wheelwright sat down at last. He had no idea who the murderer might be. The only thing of which he seemed certain was that it would make no difference what the truth was: Titus's friends would all stick together and their slaves would say whatever they were told to say. This was offered more as a statement of fact than a complaint, and Ruso had no doubt he was right.

The prompt of "Tell me about Titus" brought a less honest assessment. Contrary to Flora's account, it seemed the dead youth had been full of promise: clever, lively, obviously destined for high office.

"Did you like him?"

"It wasn't my business to like him."

At least he hadn't lied. "I'm told you were brothers."

Verax nodded. "My mother was a slave. His mother was the wife." He looked up. "I wasn't jealous of him, sir. Who'd want to live like that?"

"Like what?"

The young man rubbed his unshaven chin, apparently struggling to find words. Finally he said, "He was never allowed to do anything useful."

Tilla said, "Why did you talk about hurting him?"

Verax jerked round to face her. "Who told you that?" The lamp flame reflected in the dark eyes as he looked from one to the other of them. "It was just talk," he said. "I wouldn't have done it."

Ruso said, "What wouldn't you have done?"

"He upset Flora," Verax explained, confirming what Tilla had said earlier. "I went to see him in private and told him if he ever went near her again I'd break his nose."

Ruso said, "And?"

"He never bothered her again, and I kept away from him."

Tilla's question of "What about other girls? Did he bother them?" seemed to cause him some difficulty. Finally he said, "See, I thought, last night... only he wasn't." He cleared his throat. "It turns out there's a lot more to driving than just driving."

They finally untangled the events of the party from a confused account that was punctuated with "I know nobody will believe this."

Tilla said, "But why did you try to pull the girl away?"

"Because I'm a fool, miss."

"You do not seem like a fool to me," she told him. "And I think Flora would not waste her time with you if you were."

The young man shrugged awkwardly, as if embarrassed by the compliment. "It sounds stupid now," he said. "But I thought that this Xanthe might be—you know, a decent girl who'd had too much wine. And that

Titus was taking advantage of her. Then when she told Titus to get rid of me I thought she must be a hanger-on wanting a ride out to the estate so she could play at being rich. But she was just one of the girls they hire for parties, earning a living."

Tilla said, "So you were doing your best to look after them both."

Verax mumbled, "I suppose." He glanced up. "I didn't make a very good job of it, did I?"

"I am sure you tried to do the right thing," Tilla assured him.

"Titus was very young," Verax said suddenly. "And not as clever as he thought he was."

"You are the older brother?"

He nodded. In the pause that followed he glanced at the door again. "I was hoping Flora might find me something to eat."

Tilla promised to go and see what was in the kitchen in a moment.

Ruso was not sure he shared his wife's sympathy. What if the man were just a plausible liar? He said, "Who helped you escape this afternoon?"

The dark head jerked up. "Nobody, sir."

"You got past the locks yourself?"

"Yes, sir." There was a slight pause before, "Really."

"Fortune must have been kind to you," Ruso observed, choosing not to demand how, exactly, he had gone about picking the locks.

Verax had recovered enough to look him in the eye. "I wanted to see your sister, sir."

At least that much was true. As was the fact that Verax was a hopeless liar and was obviously trying to defend whoever had let him out.

Tilla said, "Where will you go?"

"A long way from here," he told her. "Wherever I can get work."

"In the meantime," Ruso put in, "the person who murdered your brother will get away with it."

"Sir, nobody else is going to be accused. The kitchen girl told everyone she found me standing over Titus with the jug still in my hand."

Tilla said, "That girl needs to be properly questioned."

Verax shook his head. "That's what she saw." Catching Ruso's eye, he added, "I thought he'd fallen down drunk, sir. The jug was lying on top of him. I was moving it so it didn't get broken when I pulled him up."

"You're sure nobody saw you hit him?"

"I didn't hit him!" Before Ruso could reply Verax lifted his hands in a gesture of surrender. "Sorry, sir," he said. "But if the regular driver hadn't sprained his wrist, I'd never have been there. And I wouldn't be here begging to say goodbye to Flora. I'd be asking to marry her."

"I'm afraid that's out of the question."

"I know."

"Unless..."

The young man looked up.

"You have a choice," Ruso told him. "You can take the risk of trying to clear your name, or you can run."

"You think I could—"

"You can hide here for one more night while we try to find out the truth. If you make any attempt to contact my sister while you're here, I'll have you taken straight back to Sabinus's estate in chains. Understood?"

"Understood." For the first time, Verax's face cracked

into something like a smile. "Thank you, sir."

Ruso glanced at his wife, saw the warmth of her expression and realized to his annoyance that Flora's unlucky choice was the sort of youth whom women found irresistibly handsome.

10

This morning's search was not going as well as Tilla had hoped. The shady side-streets of Nemausus had turned to airless ovens in the time she and Marcia had been tramping around them. She had paused so many times to slake her thirst from dented cups chained to corner fountains that she now felt bloated as well as hot. In truth she was ceasing to care whether anyone here knew how to find a girl called Xanthe: she was more interested in finding a cool place to sit down. Marcia, who had begun by being keen to help, was growing more and more uneasy about being seen with a foreigner who was accosting brothel doorkeepers. Especially after one man had included both of them in his glance when he said, "Looking for work, girls?"

Now, slumped against a wall in a narrow strip of shade, Marcia pulled her stole forward to hide more of her face and said, "How much longer are we supposed to keep this up? If anyone at home finds out, I'm going to have a lot of explaining to do. We should have brought some slaves so we look respectable."

"Then everyone at home would be sure to find out." Tilla bent to ease a piece of grit out of her sandal. "There must be places we haven't tried."

"This could take days. She probably has a new name with every client. You might never find her."

It was *you* now, Tilla noticed, not *we*.

"Even if you do," Marcia continued, "why would she tell you anything?"

Tilla busied herself with the strap of the sandal, because she did not know the answer. Nor could she explain to Marcia how urgent this was, because Marcia would want to know why, and she could not say, *Because your brother says Verax can only hide in your bathhouse until tomorrow*. Once she had got over her surprise that Verax was there at all, Marcia would ask why he couldn't stay longer, and Tilla did not want to say, *Because your brother is trying to ride two horses at once*. The workings of her husband's mind were a mystery she did not wish to discuss.

The argument had started early this morning after he came back from taking Verax some bread and goat's cheese. "Swear to me, Tilla," he said, taking her by the arm in the privacy of Flora's bedroom, "you won't tell anybody he's here."

She said, "I will not tell anybody."

That should have been enough for him, but he carried on. "Especially Flora," he said.

"Not even Flora."

"And you won't get anyone else to tell her."

"Husband, I have already sworn!"

"And you won't try to make sure she finds out."

She shook his hand off her arm. "What makes you think I will do any of these things?"

"Experience."

She turned her back and carried on plaiting her hair, but he did not take the hint.

"I know you do whatever you think best back in Britannia, Tilla, but things are different here."

"I see."

"If it wasn't Verax who killed that boy, it was one of Titus's friends or their staff. They're probably all from wealthy families, and if they get the idea we're out to trap them, they could make a lot of trouble for us."

She said, "If you do not trust me to help, perhaps you would like to go and look for this Xanthe yourself."

"Would you like me to?"

"No."

So that had not been a good way to begin the day. Then her mother-in-law had grabbed them both as they were leaving for town and announced that now Lucius was not here to worry about it—your brother is such a worrier, dear!—she was going to send a couple of the staff across to open up the bathhouse and light the furnace. She was not pleased to be told that it wasn't a good idea.

"But dear, you travelled all that way, and you can't have bathed for days! You aren't worried about what Lucius will say, are you? Just do what I do, dear, and don't let him bother you. You know how hopeless he is with money. It really can't cost that much. The slaves are here already and the wood—"

"Tomorrow," Ruso had told her. "We're taking Marcia shopping today."

"Shopping?" Her face brightened. "Does Flora know? I'll call her. It will take her mind off—"

From inside the house came a cry of, "I'm not going shopping, Mother! What *is* the matter with you all?"

"In any case, dear," Arria continued, ignoring her daughter's scorn, "the hot room will take all day to warm up. Then it'll be ready when you—"

"I'm going to the baths in town. I have to meet someone."

That had distracted her. “Someone interesting?”

“Actually, yes. A man who knows all about gallstones.”

“Gallstones? Oh, Gaius!” She sighed. “We’ll do it tomorrow, then.”

“After I’ve inspected the building,” he told her. “It’ll need looking over before we fire it back up. I had a patient in Britannia whose hot-room floor collapsed when they lit the furnace after a long break. He had some very nasty burns.”

Tilla hoped the threat of a collapsing bath floor—something she had never heard of before today—would keep Verax safely hidden until he was proven innocent. But so far her own efforts to help by finding Xanthe were going nowhere. Marcia, here to fetch help if Tilla disappeared for too long inside one of the brothels, was turning out to be more of a burden than a—

“Quintus!” cried Marcia, suddenly finding the energy to pull herself away from the wall and fling up her hands in delight at the sight of a slightly overweight young man stepping out of a building they had just visited.

“Marcia?” The young man looking up from fastening his belt seemed more startled than pleased.

“We haven’t seen you for ages!” Marcia went on. “How’s the family?”

The family, it seemed, was well. The baby was almost a month old now and thriving. Quintus, edging away, apologized for being in a hurry to get home to them.

“Well, it was lovely to see you,” Marcia assured him. “I’ll come and visit Silvia and the baby very soon.” She squinted up at the position of the sun. “Perhaps I could come now. Would that be all right?”

Quintus’s throat moved as he swallowed. Before he

could reply she went on, "I suppose we ought to get our story straight first, though. Does Silvia mind that you're visiting prostitutes?"

The chin rose. "There's nothing wrong with it."

"No of course not," Marcia assured him. "A healthy man has needs. Especially when his wife's busy with a baby, although I must say if I caught my husband at it, he'd be sorry. I'm glad she's so understanding."

"I am told, sister," put in Tilla, "that for a Roman man there is no shame in having to buy the company of women. Your friend can do as he pleases."

"Of course he can," Marcia agreed. "I expect most wives don't mind at all. In fact some might say it was being considerate."

Quintus cleared his throat. "It's not a very good time to call," he tried. "Silvia's probably still asleep. The baby, you know. Night and day. It's very tiring."

Marcia appeared to ponder this for a moment. "Actually," she said, "I do have something else I'm supposed to be doing this morning, and you might be able to help. Go back in and tell them a friend is organising a party and he wants to know where he can find Xanthe."

Quintus frowned. "But—"

"If I can find Xanthe," Marcia explained, "I'll be too busy to come and talk to Silvia." Watching Quintus's retreating back as he hurried into the brothel Marcia observed, "I still don't know what Silvia sees in him. He's got the brains of a brush."

11

The room was tiny, but someone had swathed the walls with fabrics that were dyed sunshine yellow and sky blue and looked surprisingly like silk. A polished bronze mirror hung on a nail by the window and beneath it, a small table held a jumble of bottles and mixing-pots, hairpins and soft goat-hair brushes. On the edge sat a little brass make-up grinder dusted with red powder, and a wooden comb with several teeth missing. Xanthe must be a valuable slave to have not only the luxury of a room all to herself, but also so many costly things to fill it with.

Tilla perched in the only space between piles of clothes on the narrow bed, and said, "It is good of you to talk to me."

Xanthe, standing above her, paused in the selection of earrings from a pot on the table. "Poor Titus," she murmured, closing delicately-painted eyes as if trying to shut out the memory. "Murdered by his own driver. I saw the whole thing. It was terrible."

"By his driver?" Tilla swallowed, hoping her disappointment did not show. Things had been going so well until now. They had finally found where Xanthe lived, the hulking doorman had let her in as soon as she said her sister-in-law knew Titus, and Xanthe seemed keen to tell what she knew. But what she knew was not at all what Tilla wanted to hear.

"It all happened so quickly," Xanthe continued.

Tilla said, "I am surprised that anyone would dare to do such a thing at a party."

A blue glass droplet set in silver dangled from between the girl's finger and thumb. "It was dark," she said. "And there was a lot going on. I expect the driver thought nobody was looking." She leaned sideways to peer into the mirror so she could guide the earring into position. "Tell your sister-in-law that it was very quick. Titus wouldn't have known much about it."

Tilla said, "Perhaps that will be a comfort," as if Flora was likely to care. "So you saw just one blow?"

Xanthe raised her right arm, pale fist clenched around an invisible handle. "The driver lifted up the jug like this..." She swung the arm down, "and smacked it onto poor Titus's head."

Tilla said, "Oh."

Xanthe positioned a necklace against her throat and turned away, head bowed and the two ends held out behind her. "Fasten that for me, will you?"

Tilla guided the silver hook through the ring and laid it against the smooth skin. She was surprised at how changed the girl looked once the jewellery was in place. Unadorned, she could have been no more than fifteen. Now she looked harder, and older, and much less vulnerable. "It was bad luck for the killer that somebody saw what happened," she said.

"The driver pulled Titus round behind the carriage," said Xanthe, with less hesitation than Tilla would have liked. "By the wall, where he thought nobody could see them. And then..." She demonstrated the killing blow once more.

"I heard Titus was found inside the carriage?"

Xanthe squinted into the mirror again and adjusted a strand of hair against the fine line of her cheekbone before speaking. "He fell into the carriage," she said.

"Then what happened?"

"I called for help, but nobody took any notice. There was too much going on. Then the driver said if I didn't shut up he'd hit me, too."

This was getting worse and worse. "What about the other girls?" Tilla tried. "Did they see anything?"

"I don't know."

"They have said nothing to you?" Tilla was surprised.

"I don't know them. Publius hired them from somewhere else."

"I must try and find them," Tilla mused. "Can you remember any names?"

The neatly-plucked eyebrows gathered into a frown. "I've told you what happened," she said. "Titus and his driver had an argument in front of everybody. Later on the driver grabbed hold of Titus, pulled him out of sight and smacked him on the head with the jug. There isn't anything else." She looked sidelong at Tilla. "I'm only telling you this because they caught him anyway. They won't send men to question me, will they?"

Tilla, who had no idea whether questioners would be sent or not, said, "You have been a great help. No-one is accusing you of anything. We just want to know the truth."

"Poor Titus."

"Do you know what he and the driver argued about?"

"Oh, you know." Xanthe waved a hand vaguely in the air. "Titus was a bit drunk, to be honest."

"Was the driver drunk too?"

"Maybe. He was behaving oddly."

"Really?"

Xanthe paused to select a hairpin from the pot on the table. "If your sister-in-law was sweet on Titus, she might not want to hear this."

Tilla said, "I might not tell her."

"Fair enough. It was when Titus was taking me into the carriage for some fun. The driver took it into his head to try and stop me. I've never seen a slave overstep himself that far before. I mean, Titus was his master! What was he thinking?"

"But Verax is not—"

"Verax?"

Tilla was unable to stop herself any longer. "The driver. He's a freedman. He is not Titus's real driver. He is just an estate worker who was helping out. He did not know who you were, but he did know that Titus had a bad name for seducing girls. He thought you might regret it later."

Xanthe put the hairpin down. "Who are you, exactly?"

"Verax was trying to protect you."

"Protect me?"

"Yes," said Tilla. "And now he is accused of murder."

Xanthe swallowed. "Well he shouldn't have done it then, should he?"

"He says he didn't do it. My sister-in-law is heartbroken. She was hoping to marry him."

"Marry the driver? You told me she was a friend of Titus!"

"I told you she knew Titus," Tilla reminded her.

While she tried to explain, Xanthe reached one foot under the table and slid out a fancy sandal. "I need to go." Xanthe slipped the sandal on and groped for its twin.

"And you can get out too."

"Xanthe, please. Did Verax really—"

"I've said everything I have to say." The girl leaned across to drag open the door. "Go."

12

The slave with the squint hurried away, and Ruso was left to wait under the open roof of the atrium with only the little figurines of the household gods watching him from their shrine in the corner. He had never called on Publius before, but the house was familiar from the visits he and his brother had made to discuss repayment of the family debt to Publius's father.

A servant scurried across the hallway. Ruso wondered whether Publius's promised questioning of the staff was over, and whether it had achieved anything apart from a further widening of the gulf between master and slaves.

The sound of footsteps caused him to look up, but it was only another servant passing along a wooden balcony that led to the upstairs rooms. Ruso supposed the staircase—wherever it was—must be the one down which Publius's sister had fallen. Or, according to Marcia, been pushed.

Even without hearing the gossip he would have guessed that all was not running smoothly in the Germanicus household. Beside him, an elegantly-painted screen depicting a garden had a broken hinge held together with fresh twine, and a similar repair had been carried out on a cracked pot holding one of the plants fringing the traditional rainwater pool. In the pool itself a drift of fallen leaves had gathered in one corner, and amongst them were what looked like shards of broken glass. Either the household was still recovering from a rambunctious party, or standards had gone down since his last visit.

Ruso eyed the heavily-studded treasure chest that held pride of place at the centre of the far wall. It was a fancier version of the one in his father's study, and there was no way of knowing what was in there. He hoped Publius wasn't planning to increase the loan repayments to help with the cost of household repairs.

A door in the corner opened and a burly man strode out clutching a leather purse. The slave with the squint hurried in to speak with his master, and moments later Publius emerged. He looked a great deal more comfortable in a cream tunic than he had in yesterday's cumbersome toga.

"Gaius Petreius?" He showed no sign of remembering Ruso from their meeting beside Titus's bier. "My secretary tells me you're the brother of Lucius. A very reliable man."

It was an encouraging start. "Thank you, sir. He's away at the moment. I was hoping to pay my respects to your father while I'm home. I'm very sorry to hear it's too late."

"Thank you."

"And my sister Marcia asked me to send her good wishes to your own sister after her accident."

A frown clouded the handsome features. "My sister is making a good recovery. And your family are...?"

"All well, thank you, sir."

Publius said, "Ah," and then, "Good."

"I'm just passing through on the way from Rome to

Britannia," said Ruso, largely in order to make some sort of noise while he was searching for a tactful way to turn the conversation to, *I hear a man was murdered in your garden*. He should have been thinking about that while he was waiting, instead of musing about staircases and money-chests and flowerpots.

"And how are things in Rome?"

What sort of a question was that? Publius was evidently no better than he was himself at making idle conversation. "Busy, sir."

"I'm thinking of going there myself shortly. I know a few people who can introduce me."

"I'm sure you'll do well, sir."

Publius, having led the conversation down this alley, did not seem to know how to steer it back out again. He turned to the man with the squint. "Is there anything I need to discuss with Gaius Petreius?"

"All the business arrangements are running smoothly, sir."

Something about the way Publius said, "Excellent," reminded Ruso of a much older man. As if the lad was trying to imitate the dead father. An idea began to form, but already Publius was moving away as if the meeting was over.

Ruso said, "Your father and mine were good friends, sir, so if there's anything I can do to help at this difficult time—"

I'll let you know. It was good of you to call."

"I know when my own father died the administration seemed endless." Especially when the debts had come to light, but he had no intention of dwelling on that. "And that was before I realized it was my job to find suitable husbands for my sisters."

Suddenly the young man was paying attention. "What?"

"While I'm here, sir, there's a private matter that I'd like to discuss with you."

Publius's expression was somewhere between annoyance and alarm. "I hope you aren't intending to mention my sister."

"Absolutely not, sir." Too late, it occurred to Ruso that it sounded as if he had come here to propose. "It's my own sister I'm concerned about."

"I see."

"Not Marcia," he added. "She's already married. Flora."

Publius did not look mollified. "Are you suggesting that I might want to marry one of your sisters?"

"No!" This was getting worse by the moment. "No, sir. I'd like to talk about the young man Flora was hoping to marry. He was here the other night."

The young heir glanced at his man, who shook his head. "I don't think so."

"He was Titus's driver, sir."

The effect was like jabbing a needle into an inflated bladder. Ruso watched as the outraged defender of his sister's honour sank into a man with the weight of responsibility on his shoulders.

"A terrible thing," Publius said. "Terrible. And in this house!"

"Ghastly," Ruso agreed. No wonder Publius was thinking of making a fresh start in Rome. "I realize it's out of both our hands, sir, but—well to be honest, Flora is heartbroken. I promised her I'd do what I could."

"I'm not sure how I can help. You need to talk to Sabinus."

“I’ve spoken to him, sir, and I gather you were having your staff questioned.” If Publius wanted to conclude—wrongly—that Ruso had the old man’s blessing to interfere, that was fine. “I’ve been hoping there might be some innocent explanation. That you might have discovered something that suggests Titus’s death was an accident.”

“And Sabinus knows about this?”

“He does, sir.”

Publius sighed. “I’d like to think it was an accident. Poor old Titus had had rather a skinful, to be honest. None of us was entirely sober. If my kitchen maid hadn’t seen the driver there, we might have thought he’d just fallen over and knocked his head. But I had her questioned last night—which wasn’t pleasant for any of us, by the way—and she’s sticking to her story. Actually, why don’t I call her?” Publius glanced at his slave, who nodded and slipped away. “You can ask her yourself.”

While the maid was being fetched, Publius led Ruso through double doors into a corridor where glassless windows opened onto sunlit rose beds beyond. “I hope this won’t take too long,” he said, leading Ruso outside. “Obviously it’s painful for everyone.”

Almost immediately, a thin girl with mousy hair appeared. She stopped on the far side of the nearest flower bed with her gaze fixed on her master’s feet, and bowed. Her hands were clutched together in a futile attempt to stop them shaking. Her tunic was spattered with stains in places where an apron had failed to reach. Slightly to one side of her, Ruso noticed that the stone Bacchus on a plinth had an arm missing and what seemed to be a fresh break where his nose should have been.

Publius said, "This man is here to find out what happened to my friend Titus."

The girl clasped her hands tighter and nodded a little too eagerly.

"He's not going to hurt you." Publius cast a glance at Ruso as if seeking his agreement.

"Certainly not," Ruso told her.

"No-one will hurt you any more as long as you tell the truth. I want you to tell him exactly what you saw."

The girl shuffled her feet and said nothing.

"Well?"

"Yes, sir."

"Speak up, girl!"

She gulped. "I—I—" A tear slid to the end of her nose and dripped down her tunic. Then another one.

"Stop crying!" ordered Publius.

Ruso, who had never known this order to achieve the desired result, said, "May I ask her some questions?"

Publius gave a "be my guest" gesture. "If you don't know the answer," he told the girl, "just say so. Don't make anything up, and don't leave anything out."

The girl's account was interrupted by sniffing and it was not fluent, but it was consistent. She had come out of the kitchen, looked across the courtyard and seen a pair of feet sticking out of the carriage door. She had gone to see if it was a guest who needed help. When she got there she had seen young master Titus's slave standing over him with something in his hand.

"Like this." She demonstrated by raising one fist above her head while bending over an imaginary victim. "And the young master was lying all..." She unclasped her hands just enough to move them in parallel as if they were trying to straighten something. "All wrong, sir."

"What was his man holding?"

"A wine jug, sir."

"And then?"

"The man shouted at me. And then everyone came."

"What did he shout?"

"It wasn't me."

Ruso nodded. "What were you doing out in the courtyard with the guests?"

The girl gave a double sniff.

"Tell him," sighed Publius. "And blow your nose. That sniffing is disgusting."

The girl glanced around as if wondering how to obey, then resorted to hauling up the neckline of her tunic. "Cook said to come. There was a—a—"

"A commotion," supplied Publius.

"In case the master needed help seeing the guests out."

"And you came through that door you just used?"

She indicated the service door that was almost hidden behind the ruined Bacchus. "Yes, sir."

"So Titus's carriage was where?"

"Over there, sir." She pointed to a broad paved area beyond the flower beds, accessible by a tall pair of gates in the back wall.

"Facing which way?"

She pointed at the gates.

"Towards the street," explained Publius.

"Then what happened?"

The girl risked a glance at her master, who said, "Answer the question."

"I don't know, sir. Cook said to find the kitchen boy to fetch the doctor."

Ruso nodded. "I see. You've been very helpful. Thank

you. Just one last question. Did you actually see anyone strike Titus?"

"Tell the truth," urged her master.

She shook her head. "No, sir."

Dismissed, the girl almost blundered into Bacchus in her haste to get back to the safety of the kitchen.

Ruso turned to Publius. "What happened to the driver after that?"

"My people locked him in a storeroom," Publius explained. "Then we sent for Sabinus's people, as I'm sure you know." He scratched his head. "It was dreadful, frankly. I've never had to deal with anything like this before. And my first thought was, I'll ask Pa. He'll know what to do."

"I'm sure you did everything you could," said Ruso, unable to recall a time when he would have sought his father's advice about anything.

"Between you and me," Publius murmured, "the staff were very shaken. Some of them were refusing to come out here again. I had to have priests around yesterday to purify the place."

Ruso said, "It would help to speak to anyone else who was at the party."

Publius frowned. "There were some hired girls."

"I was thinking of the other guests. If you could tell me—"

"I've already asked them. The kitchen maid is the only one who saw anything."

"They may have seen something that they didn't think was important at the time," Ruso explained. "Something that might be useful."

Publius still looked doubtful. "It was a private party, you know. I'm not sure my friends would want—"

"It's a tragic business for old Sabinus," Ruso reminded him. "The whole family must have had high hopes for the boy. Especially since he's related to the senator."

The relationship to the senator was not close, but the mere mention of it was like oiling a lock. "I suppose I could introduce you," Publius conceded. "Most of them are probably at the baths." He turned back to the house. "Let's get it over with, then."

13

The marbled splashiness of Nemausus's town baths was a sharp contrast with the dank, abandoned facilities at home. Even when the late bath boy had been doing his best, the family had regularly complained that he didn't change the water often enough. It was easier to blame the slave than to admit that the whole scheme (another of Ruso's stepmother's ideas) had been over-ambitious: that if there wasn't enough water to run a fountain, there certainly wasn't enough for a bathhouse. Whereas here, fresh water flowing from distant hills was piped into the town day and night. It fed an abundance of gleaming pools and tumbling water features, including the sparkling fountain beneath which three young men sat cooling their feet.

All three were fashionably bearded and although Publius introduced them by name, Ruso could not help thinking of them as Bushy, Wispy and Patchy.

When Publius told them that Ruso had come to ask about the party, each young man in turn offered his own version of "Poor old Titus." On learning that Ruso's sister had been hoping to marry Titus's driver, Patchy said, "Ouch," and the others winced.

"Exactly." Ruso chose a place next to the heavy figure of Bushy, and bent to untie his sandals.

"Poor old Titus," repeated Patchy as Publius settled

beside him.

Wispy said, "Anything we can do to help. All you have to do is ask."

"I'm not sure we can do very much, really," put in Patchy as Ruso submerged his feet in the welcome chill. "By the time poor old Titus was found, we'd all left. I had no idea anything was wrong until the message arrived the next day."

"Nor me," agreed Wispy. "We were all a bit the worse for wear at the time."

Publius said, "I never invited any of you in the first place."

"That was why we came," Patchy told him. "We heard you were stuck at home all by yourself feeling miserable. We came to cheer you up."

"So it was a good evening?" asked Ruso, whose idea of a good party was one he didn't have to go to.

"Till old Publius here threw us out," said Patchy, sounding almost proud of it.

"And Titus enjoyed himself, as far as you know?"

"Absolutely," Patchy assured him. He turned to his friends. "Wasn't it him who suggested the hunt? With that girl—what was her name?"

"Xanthe," put in Wispy.

"That's the one. Wearing that—whatever she was wearing."

"Not very much."

"I had the one with the tits, you had her friend and Titus had Xanthe."

Ruso said, "Hunt?"

Patchy indicated the stolid form of Bushy, who had not said a word since expressing his regrets about the death. "And he had the—what was it?"

"A very expensive antique silver cup," put in Publius.

"Really? It didn't look expensive. Anyway, whoever has the cup, or whatever, is the stag. So he has to run, and everyone else counts to twenty and grabs a girl and the girls ride around—on us, obviously—and try to find him and snatch the cup off him. Then whoever's girl gets the cup is the next stag."

"I see," said Ruso.

"It's a game," explained Wispy. "It's fun."

"Yes," said Ruso, feeling very old.

"Until things get broken," said Publius.

"Yes, well..." conceded Patchy. But if Publius was expecting an apology, he was disappointed. The nearest he got was, "It did get a bit out of hand. But we only wanted to cheer you up. If you don't mind me saying, brother, you've become very serious lately. I'm worried about you."

"We've all noticed," agreed Wispy.

"I'm busy," Publius told them. "Now Pa's gone I have masses of business to get through every day. People come visiting at ridiculous hours of the morning. I can't be up half the night like you lot."

"That's why we left early when you asked," Patchy told him.

"After about the fifth time of asking," Publius growled.

"You did get a bit agitated," Patchy agreed. "But it wasn't just us. It was Titus as well. You know what he's—well, what he was like."

Ruso said, "What was he like?"

Titus, it seemed, had always gone a bit too far, and a recent spell as some sort of junior official in Rome had not improved things. "I heard he got sent back early,"

Patchy admitted. “Of course when he got back he was a bit *everything's-better-in-Rome*, you know? But he never said much about what he actually did there. I heard his pa was trying to find a legion that would take him so he couldn't get into any more trouble.”

It was clear to Ruso that neither Sabinus nor Patchy had ever served in a legion.

“He wasn't always as funny as he thought he was,” agreed Wispy. “But that's no reason for his driver to kill him. It just goes to show, you can't trust slaves. Not deep down. They're different from us.”

“They are,” agreed Patchy. “My grandfather had a man who was brought up on the farm and they'd known him all his life and always been fair with him. Then they found out he'd been stealing from them for years, and when my grandfather confronted him the fellow went for him with a kitchen knife.”

Ruso restrained the urge to point out that this was irrelevant since Verax wasn't a slave. Or at least, not any more. But they would probably explain that you couldn't trust freedmen either. So instead he said, “Did you all have your own people there, waiting to take you home?”

“All the visiting staff were out in the courtyard.” Publius glanced at his friends. “We ought to have them questioned.”

Ruso said, “Or I could just ask them—”

“Oh, it's no good you talking to them,” Patchy insisted. “They'll all be sympathetic to the driver. They won't tell you anything. It needs to be somebody who isn't involved.”

“Or somebody who knows them well enough to tell when they're lying,” said Wispy. He turned to Ruso. “We could ask them for you and tell Publius what they say.”

It was frustrating, but not unexpected, and Ruso moved on. "Has anybody spoken to the hired girls?"

This time Publius said, "Perhaps you should try."

"I've just thought of something!" declared Patchy suddenly. He looked around the group, waiting until he had everyone's attention. "Listen. Did anybody see Titus after the hunt went into the garden?"

He was met with a row of blank faces.

"Publius?"

"I can't remember."

"Because I think I saw him getting into his carriage again with the girl. I took no notice at the time. But I don't remember seeing him after that."

There was a pause, then it was agreed that nobody else had seen them after that either.

"I think I saw them by the carriage too," Wispy put in. "Just after me and what's-her-name got there." He frowned. "Wasn't Titus waving a wine jug about on the hunt?"

"It would be just like him," said Patchy. "If there was something left in it."

There was a murmur of agreement, then a silence broken only by the trickle of the fountain and the shouts of youths playing a ball game over in the exercise area.

Ruso said, "When did the girls leave?"

"They were hanging about afterwards," Publius told him, a hard edge in his voice. "They hadn't been paid."

"Really?" put in Wispy. "That's a bit rich. Asking for money when poor old Titus is lying there with his brains bashed in."

"They didn't know that at the time," Publius pointed out. "As soon as we found him they went away."

"Without their money?" Patchy's eyebrows rose. "So

it was a cheap evening."

"No it wasn't," Publius snapped. "I don't want my name all over town as a host who doesn't pay his bills. I sent my man out the next morning to settle up, and now you three owe me."

Evidently humbled by his tone, the bearded trio all immediately assured him that they would pay up, although only Bushy seemed to be carrying any money. He was prevailed upon to reimburse Publius, since that was only fair, and the other two promised to pay him back just as soon as they had the cash.

"Maybe it wasn't the driver after all." Bushy's sole contribution to the interview was the one Ruso had wanted to hear.

"You know," put in Patchy, "I think it could have been the girl."

"Even so," Wispy pointed out, "the driver should have protected him."

His friend ignored the interruption. "Maybe Titus took her in there for another go, and she didn't want to."

"It's possible," Wispy agreed. "Women are temperamental. And like I said, you can't trust slaves. They don't—"

Whatever he might have said was interrupted by the approach of a bath attendant, presumably one of the class of people who were not to be trusted. He came close enough not to draw attention from the other bathers and said, "Sirs, no feet in the fountain, please."

Wispy lunged down into the water and splashed it over his friends. "Feet out of the fountain, boys!"

"You get yours out!" cried Patchy, splashing him back. "What are you? A barbarian?"

Ruso retreated, wiping water out of his eyes. The

slave stood and watched as Publius climbed out and Bushy glanced around before following them.

"Sirs—"

"We're just going," Patchy assured the slave, pausing to give Wispy one last soaking before they both scrambled out.

14

Tilla wished her husband would hurry up and finish talking to those men over by the fountain. She was hot and sticky even here under the shade of the snack bar canopy, and she was brooding on Xanthe's damning testimony. She needed to share it with someone, but that someone was not Marcia. Even though Marcia had given her half of a raisin pastry and then insisted that she had a right to be told. Tilla had eked out the pastry for as long as possible, but even the sparrows hopping around their feet had given up searching for the last crumbs and gone to another table. So now the two of them were sitting at opposite ends of a bench, with Tilla pretending to be interested in a noisy ball game on the far side of the exercise area, and Marcia muttering that she hoped nobody knew she was related to one of those idiots over there with his big feet in the fountain.

"At last!" Marcia announced as a childish water fight broke out and the group of men split up.

Tilla stood and waved, and her husband strolled across to join them, carrying his sandals and shaking water out of his hair.

"You wouldn't believe what we've had to put up with this morning," Marcia told him. "Tilla was inside one of those disgusting places for so long I nearly had to go in myself and get her. Anyway, I found your girl for you, and now Tilla's going to tell us what she said."

He said, "Publius says to tell you his sister is making a good recovery."

"Did he look guilty about pushing her down the stairs?"

"Not especially."

"I might go and visit her," said Marcia. "I could ask what she's heard about the murder. I bet the staff would tell her things they wouldn't tell Publius."

Tilla and her husband exchanged a glance.

"You could come too," Marcia added. "Pretend to check her for broken bones, or something."

He frowned. "It's a bit late to—"

"I will come," Tilla put in, not because she thought the girl would want to see either of them, but because she could see another argument brewing. She need not have worried: at that moment a small boy arrived to tell Marcia the foot masseur was ready for her.

"Good!" Marcia snatched up her bag and stood holding out one hand to Ruso. "I'll need enough for the hairdresser as well."

Ruso said, "If you can't afford it, why did you arrange it?"

"Because I knew you'd want to thank me for all I've done for you."

He hesitated just long enough to show his annoyance before paying. Watching her departing figure, he said, "What does she need her feet massaged for?"

"I have news for you, husband."

"It's not as if she ever walks anywhere."

"It is not good news."

"Well, I suppose it'll buy us some peace." He lowered himself onto Marcia's end of the bench with what sounded like a sigh of satisfaction. "I've had a productive morning."

"The girl Xanthe saw everything."

"Really?"

She slid closer so they could not be overheard by the other customers. When she had finished telling him what Xanthe had said, he said, "Are you sure that's exactly it? Behind the carriage where nobody could see, and Titus fell inside the door?"

"That is exactly it. She is sure it was Verax."

He thought for a moment, then said, "Good."

"How can it be good?" Had she not made it plain? "She saw—"

"I heard what you said." He folded his arms and looked very pleased with himself. "But that isn't what she saw."

"But—" Tilla stopped. "You think she is wrong?"

"I saw the carriage yesterday on the estate, and I stood in Publius's courtyard this morning. It can't have happened the way she told you. The carriage door is on the wrong side. I think she's lying."

Tilla said, "Oh."

"I've just been talking to Titus's friends. They say he was with Xanthe shortly before he was killed. One of them saw them getting into the carriage together, and nobody saw him afterwards. What does that suggest to you?"

"We already know they were in the carriage together," she reminded him. "Verax told us he tried to stop them."

"This was later. They were all out in the courtyard playing some sort of game that involved running around in pairs. The friends are going to find out if any of their slaves saw anything useful, and report back to Publius."

"I see," Tilla said. And then, "It is a pity. I liked her."

"We won't tell Flora the details yet, but we can tell her it's looking hopeful."

Flora. Tilla had almost forgotten why they were doing this. "I did wonder why Xanthe was speaking to me," she mused. "Verax was already accused. She could have said she saw nothing and stayed out of it."

"When you arrived asking questions she must have panicked. Probably guessed she'd been seen by the carriage with Titus. She was throwing dust in your eyes."

"Why would a hired girl attack a client in a house where everyone knew who she was?"

He shrugged. "Who knows why someone like that would do anything?"

She turned to stare at him. "Are you asking that because she is a woman, or a slave, or a prostitute?"

"I'm sorry if you liked her, wife, but *somebody* did it. She was seen there, and she's lied about what happened."

"But what reason could she—"

"Maybe Titus did something nasty to her earlier."

Tilla lifted her skirts to fan some air around her feet. The story still did not make sense. "If I was Xanthe," she said, "and a man did something nasty to me at a party, I would get away from him as fast as possible."

"Well you aren't," he said. "Thank the gods."

"If I needed to kill him I would do it later."

"That's reassuring."

"It would be safer," she explained. "Not so much danger of being caught."

"Whatever the girl's reasons, it's good news for Flora." He glanced back over his shoulder to where the snack-vendor was wiping a grubby cloth along the counter. "Have we got time for a drink before Marcia comes back?"

"The masseur is a very handsome young Greek," she told him. "And then there is the hairdresser. I think we have time for lots of drinks."

He looked pained. "I can't spend the whole afternoon hanging around here. I've got things to do."

He should have thought of that before he gave Marcia so much money, but it would not help to tell him so. Instead she said, "If you go when you are ready, I can bring her home in the cart when—" She broke off. "That man over by the barber's stall. I have seen him before."

He followed her gaze. "Publius," he told her. "The host of the party. You saw him with me at the fountain just now."

"Not him. The one with the squinty eye."

"His slave."

"I saw him leaving Xanthe's house just as we arrived. Your Publius has been sending messages to Xanthe this morning!"

Even now he was not impressed. "It was money," he said. "The girls left the party without being paid, and Publius sent him to pay up. Publius seems to be the only one of them who's got any sense of responsibility."

Tilla said, "Oh." She thought about telling him what the doorman had said as Publius's man left Xanthe's house, but he would probably have an explanation for that too, and she was tired of being told where she was wrong. "Publius's man must know how to find all the girls who were at the party," she said. "We should talk to the others as well."

He frowned. "Didn't you see them while you were there?"

"Xanthe did not know who they were." Even as she said it, it sounded foolish. And now instead of arguing, her husband was looking at her with pity and amusement, as if she were a clumsy puppy who had failed in her attempt to please.

He said gently, "I think Xanthe may have told you quite a lot that wasn't true."

She swallowed. "I will collect the cart and bring your sister home as soon as I can."

He bent down and kissed her lightly on the forehead. "I'll thank you now on Marcia's behalf," he said, "because she probably won't bother."

15

Marcia, stretched out on the massage couch in a haze of perfume and very little else, showed no interest in knowing where Tilla might be going as long she did not have to walk home. So it was easy to slip away from the baths unescorted, and hurry down the narrow, airless streets to the house where Xanthe lived.

What was not so easy was being allowed to enter. The first knock was greeted by a long silence: the second by a female voice calling, "There's someone at the door, Andreas!" The third led to a cry of "Andreas! The door!" and after a pause, the approach of footsteps. A buxom young woman with red hair and baby blue eyes looked up at Tilla and said, "Who are you?"

"I have some news for Xanthe."

"Xanthe's gone."

"When will she be back?"

"No, she's *gone*."

"I saw her here this morning!"

The girl shrugged. "Sorry."

Another voice called from inside the house, "Who is it? Where's Andreas?" and the red-haired girl called, "I think Andreas is gone too."

"What?" Footsteps came thudding down the staircase and a dark young woman appeared. One side of her hair was in ringlets and the other side was still tied up in strips of pale rag. She ran back into the house and Tilla heard her shouting for Andreas. There was some sort of conversation, then she returned and spoke one word to her companion. "Bastard."

"It might be all right. He might be—"

"I knew there was something wrong. The kitchen boy hasn't seen him either. Not since Xanthe went." The new arrival seemed to notice Tilla for the first time. "Yes?"

Neither of the girls could guess where Xanthe might have gone, and they seemed surprised that the missing doorman had gone with her. "I wouldn't mind," observed the dark one, "but he's *my* slave, not hers."

Her slave? Tilla realized with a jolt that she had read this household wrongly. She had supposed that the girls were slaves and the doorman had the job of keeping them in order on behalf of some more powerful owner. She was truly surprised to find women in charge. She thought briefly, *how foreign I have become!* But there was no time to dwell on it. "Xanthe talked to me about the party," she said. "The one where the young man was killed."

The dark girl said, "Have you come to pay us?"

So it was as she had feared: they had all been at the party, and Xanthe had lied about knowing them. She said, "I heard you had already been paid."

They glanced at each other.

"This morning," Tilla added. "Publius's man came with the money and spoke to your doorman. I saw him."

The red-haired girl stepped back to let Tilla pass. "You'd better come in."

Tilla stared around the little room in wonder. The bed she had sat on was still there, the blankets rumpled and the pillow thrown on the floor. The walls were bare apart from a torn scrap of yellow silk caught on one of the nails that scarred the dull, cracked plaster. All that was left of Xanthe's make-up was a jumble of ring-marks and blotches on the wooden surface of the table.

The red-haired girl pushed past Tilla, crouched beside the bed and eased a silver earring with a droplet of blue glass from a gap between two floorboards. "She'll be annoyed she's lost that."

"Andreas and Xanthe," muttered the dark girl. "They've taken the cash and cleared off."

"I knew something was wrong this morning," the dark girl said, looking round at the bare walls. "Somebody came to see her and she wouldn't say who it was. And then you came, and as soon as you'd gone she was packing up to go. I said, 'What about the money from the party?' and she told me when it turned up we could keep it.'"

A fly was buzzing against the windowpane. Tilla reached across and let it out, and as it flew off into the hot afternoon she made a decision.

The sound of conversation in the street faded as she closed the catch. She took a deep breath. "I am not sure I am supposed to tell you this," she said, "but people are saying it was Xanthe who killed that young man."

They both said, "Xanthe?" at the same time.

"Is that why she is gone?"

"Of course not! She wouldn't—"

The red-haired girl was grabbing at her companion's arm. "We don't know," she told Tilla.

The dark girl said, "But Xanthe wouldn't—"

"Who cares? She's gone. With our pay. There's just us left now."

The dark girl pondered that for a moment, then

turned to Tilla. "Perhaps she did do it. It's no good asking us. We don't know anything."

Tilla said, "I thought she was your friend?"

"That was before she stole Andreas and the money," said the red-haired girl.

"I came back here to warn her," said Tilla. She glanced around at the empty room. "But perhaps she has already heard what they are saying."

The red-haired girl's eyes narrowed. "Why would you warn her? You hardly know her."

Tilla shrugged. "She told me things this morning that were not true. I thought if I helped her, she might tell me the truth before her lies got her into trouble. But now she is gone, so I am asking you for the truth instead, because I do not believe she did it."

Instead of answering, the red-haired girl reached up to place her hands on Tilla's shoulders, and pressed. Tilla subsided onto the bed, trying to remember how the street door was fastened and deciding the dark girl would be the easier of the two to knock aside.

The red-haired girl said, "Listen to me, woman from across the seas who doesn't earn her living the way we do."

"I am listening."

"Then understand this. Clients get drunk and stupid at parties. They talk too much. They do things that, if they're lucky, they'll live long enough to regret. It's none of our business, and whatever we see, we don't blab about it."

"I understand."

"It's called being discreet. It's part of the job."

Tilla looked up with her best innocent face. "Did you really not see anything at all?"

The red-haired girl sighed, folded her arms and gazed down at her with the air of a disappointed parent. The other one turned away, groping in her hair for stray rags.

"I think I have been a bit of a fool," Tilla confessed. "I was so pleased when Xanthe wanted to talk to me that I never asked myself why she was doing it. And when she told me the other girls at the party lived in another place and she did not know them, I believed that, too. I did not stop to ask, *is she trying to protect her friends*?"

The red-haired girl said, "She told you she didn't know us?"

"My husband has been talking to Publius and his friends. And I can tell you, everyone is very happy to blame Xanthe." Tilla looked from one to the other of them. "If anyone comes to ask questions about that party, you will have to think very carefully what to say to them. Because if they do not think you are helping, you will be in trouble too."

The dark girl groaned. "I knew we should never have gone there."

Tilla said, "Who invited you?"

"It was Titus," said the red-haired girl. "We should have known."

"He said they would all pay us between them," put in her companion, "but they didn't. We only went because he said Publius was in charge, but I don't think Publius wanted a party at all."

"None of it was Publius's fault," observed the red-haired girl.

"He seemed a nice young man," said Tilla, who had no more than glimpsed him across the bathhouse exercise yard. "I am sorry for him."

The girls glanced at each other. The red-haired one

said, “Shall we tell her about...?”

“You just told her we were discreet.”

“But she did come to warn Xanthe.”

The dark girl turned to Tilla. “If you promise not to say where you heard it, we’ll tell you something about Publius.”

16

It struck Ruso as he set out on the long and dusty walk home that he never *wanted* to quarrel with his sisters. Yet the more reasonable he tried to be, the more exasperated they became. This time, though, would be different. This time he would be telling Flora what she wanted to hear: that there should soon be good news.

He would keep back the details until everything was sorted out, but he was certain that the girl Xanthe had incriminated herself by lying. The testimony of Bushy, Wispy and Patchy had only strengthened the case against her. With luck, some of their slaves would also have seen her in the company of Titus just before he was found dead.

As soon as all the information was gathered he would go to Sabinus and reassure the old man that he would not, after all, lose both sons at once. He would consult Sabinus about Verax's choice of bride. Then, with luck, he would be able to tell Flora the whole story, sort out her dowry and give his blessing to her marriage.

He lengthened his stride past the second milestone, shrugging some of the tension out of his shoulders. Before long all his female relatives would be happily occupied with wedding plans, and his brother would be home to run the farm. Freed from a constant barrage of demands, Ruso would have time to reintroduce his wife to the good things of his native land. Sunshine. Olives.

Wine. The absence of sulking Britons mumbling about rebellion.

Perhaps he should leave out the sulking Britons. Some of them were Tilla's family.

When he reached home there was no sign of Flora, and the laundrymaid thought she might have gone out into the vineyard. Ruso went first to the kitchen in search of a drink. He found the babyminder spooning some sort of brown mush into his daughter's mouth, while Mara was doing her best to spread it across her face and into her ears. At the sight of her father she batted the loaded spoon aside, cried "Aah!" and beamed at him, lifting both sticky arms towards him in a clear request to *pick me up!*

"In a moment." He bent to plant a kiss on a clean patch of hair before slaking his thirst with watered wine. Watching the babyminder applying a damp cloth to his protesting daughter's face and hands, it occurred to him that he and Tilla had rather neglected their responsibilities as parents over the last couple of days.

"I'll take her," he offered, and the babyminder wiped away a last smear of mush before handing her over.

"We're going for a walk," he told Mara, lifting her and tucking one arm around a pleasingly dry small bottom. "Come and see where your pa was brought up."

The cook watched them go with a fond smile. As they left, he overheard her say something to the babyminder about him being a devoted father. "Anybody would think that child was his own."

The cook might have been less impressed if she had known that the tour would give him a convenient excuse to visit Verax in the bathhouse.

The first stop on the tour, though, was the vineyard. "This," he told Mara, "is where your uncle Lucius grows the grapes to make our wine." He pointed to a tiny cluster of green nodules. "What do you think? Will it be a good year?"

When Mara did not offer an opinion he said, "No, I don't know how you tell either. Let's find your aunt Flora."

He tramped the length of the rows of vines, but there was no sign of Flora: only a couple of farm hands in rough brown tunics moving about in the dappled shade. One of them thought he had caught a glimpse of mistress Flora down in the olive grove. Meanwhile they politely referred a decision about pruning to Ruso, just as they would have to his brother. Lucius would have known the answer. As the slaves must be well aware, Ruso barely understood the question. He played along by asking them what they thought was best, and then agreed with them, leaving them to resume their work with everyone's dignity intact.

"Your ma was a slave when I met her," he told Mara. Not because she would understand, but because there were some things it was important not to forget. "You can never tell how things will turn out."

There was no sign of Flora amidst the bright scatter of poppies that bloomed beneath the gnarled olive trees. Nor was she down in the shade of the woods. He was making his way up to the house when he heard the scream of a child in pain.

Pressing Mara against him, he raced back down the slope. "Who's there? Where are you?"

A small nephew broke cover just ahead of him and fled into the trees. A second nephew staggered forward, clutching his face. Blood was dribbling out between his fingers. "My eye!" he howled. "My eye's gone!"

Mara began to cry. Ruso crouched in front of the boy. "What happened?"

"My eye!"

"Let me see."

Finally the wailing of "My eye!" subsided into frightened sobbing and the protective hand was lifted.

"Well done," Ruso told him, relieved that Mara had stopped crying in his ear. "Now let's have a look and see what's going on."

A small voice said, "Will he be all right?"

Ruso glanced up. The fugitive had returned and was standing white-faced, well out of reach.

"I didn't mean it," the boy continued. "He said, *let's throw stones*. So I did."

"Not at me, stupid!" wailed his brother. He shrank away as Ruso reached to wipe away the blood. "Will I die?"

"No," Ruso told him, glancing at Mara and wishing he too could make everything better by shoving his thumb in his mouth. "We'll go back to the house and I'll clean you up and sew you back together like I do with the soldiers."

"Will it hurt?"

He used his, "Not much," reply: the one that was a compromise between telling the truth and not frightening the patient. "I'm an expert," he added: something he would never have said to an adult. "You're lucky I'm here."

Leading his patient by the hand up the dusty path towards the house he said, "I was looking for your cousin Flora. You haven't seen her, have you?"

From behind them the smaller nephew's voice put in, "She said not to tell—" just as his injured brother said,

"Flora went for a walk."

"Where did she go?"

The younger child's voice rose. "She said we mustn't say—"

"Shut up, you!" snapped his brother. "You're in enough trouble." Then, to Ruso, "She's gone for a long walk. She said we couldn't come and we don't know where she went."

Two stitches, a cup of milk and several honey cakes later, it was apparent that the eye was in no danger. It was also apparent that the boys genuinely didn't know where Flora had gone. Ruso had a horrible suspicion that she might have headed back to Sabinus's estate, believing Verax still to be chained up over there. Well, this time she would have to manage without him. He couldn't go to retrieve her until Tilla returned from town with the family's one vehicle.

Meanwhile, though, there was someone else here who was eager to know the truth about the murder of Titus. Ruso left the boys to be fussed over by the kitchen staff while he and Mara resumed their interrupted tour of the estate.

"We'll go and look at the baths," he told Mara, heading down the corridor that led to the side door of the house. "Don't expect anything very grand," he warned her, pointing across the courtyard. "See that building over there with the render falling off and the weeds growing round the furnace? That's it. And the key is—" He stopped. The rusty nail banged into the door frame was empty.

For a moment he feared that his stepmother had ordered someone to open up the baths despite his unlikely invention of the collapsing floor. That thought was pushed aside by the more alarming possibility that Flora had gone in there for some reason, found her lover and run away with him. But a firm shove on the bathhouse door confirmed that it was still safely locked. A passing slave suggested he might ask the stable lad.

As they approached the stables, an irregular series of thunks and clatters told him someone was chopping wood. They rounded the corner to see the stable lad swing the axe down. The halves of the log skittered away in opposite directions. "I do the baths now, master," the lad explained, pausing to wipe the sweat from his forehead. "The key should be in the house. On the nail by the side door."

"But it isn't," Ruso repeated, understanding now that the lad was building up wood for the furnace. The Petreius household was not one where slaves could be kept for one task only and idle away the hours in between.

"Mistress Arria's probably taken it," suggested the lad. "Did you want to inspect the floor, master? I could ask her for the key and come with you."

"Not yet," Ruso assured him. "I'm just taking my daughter on a tour of the farm. Oh, and Tilla will be home later with the cart."

He pretended not to notice the look of alarm when the lad realized who would be driving. The beauty of having well-trained slaves was that no matter how bizarre they might find your behaviour, they never questioned it. At least, not to your face.

Ruso carried Mara into the shade of the open barn where the family carriage had once been kept. He peered up into the gloom of the cobwebbed rafters and placed a wooden box under the third beam along. Then he surveyed the dried mud floor in a vain search for somewhere clean to put the baby down. How did women manage this sort of thing? He could hardly ask the stable lad, and it seemed ridiculous to send for the babyminder. So instead he adjusted his grip, said "Hold tight!" and stepped up onto the box. Reaching above his head, he ran one hand along the dusty beam. To his delight his fingers met the rough surface of a complicated metal object.

The stable lad's eyes widened as Ruso stepped down and held out what he had found. Even with the rust and the cobwebs, it was recognizably a key to the bathhouse.

"Been up there for years," Ruso explained, proud of having proved some point he could not quite define.

The key turned with impressive ease, and Ruso pushed the door shut behind him. Empty benches stretched away into the gloom. A lone wooden bath-sandal lay in the corner and the shelves held a pile of limp-looking towels and a jumble of oil flasks and scrapers. Even on a warm day, everything smelt of damp. "This is the changing room," he told Mara, not quite sure why he was whispering.

He pushed open the next door and carried her further in, his footsteps echoing around the painted walls of what would have been the warm room if the furnace had been lit. He dabbled a couple of fingers in the cool water of the pool, sending ripples that reflected the window-light onto the painted ceiling. "There's a man in here somewhere," he whispered to Mara. "We've got some good news for him. Where do you think he is?"

The answer came in a faint snore from beyond the next door. Ruso grinned at Mara, who smiled back, displaying her latest new tooth. "Shall we go and wake him up?" He stepped up onto the stone sill, pushed the door open, and stopped dead.

For a moment he could make no sense of it. There was the naked form of Verax, revealed by the greenish light from the thick glass windows above. He was asleep face down on the wide wooden bench, and there were *too many legs*. Then there was sudden movement, and at the other end of the naked tangle Ruso found himself staring into the horrified face of his youngest sister.

"Aah!" The cry echoed around the walls as Mara smacked his arm and bounced with excitement.

"Wake up!" Flora slapped her man on the back. "Wake up!"

Verax mumbled something and snuggled deeper.

Flora's voice rose to a shriek with, "Go *away*, Gaius!"

Ruso stepped forward and grasped the furthest shoulder with one hand, rolling Verax off the bench. The young man yelled out in alarm and crashed onto the cold tiles.

Flora cried, "Don't hurt him!" as she scrambled for a towel to cover herself.

Mara stiffened in Ruso's grasp, opened her mouth and began to wail.

"Gaius, *go away*!"

Ruso took a deep breath. There were so many things he wanted to say that he did not know where to start.

If only Tilla were here. Tilla would know what to do. Meanwhile, the way that his sister's gaze lingered on the muscular nakedness of the young man reaching across the floor for a discarded tunic made him want to punch them both.

Finally he spluttered, "Put some clothes on, both of you!" and strode out of the room.

17

Mara was safely in the care of the babyminder again after a more educational tour than her father had intended. On the way back to the bathhouse he went to the gate to search in vain for any sign of Tilla's return, but it looked as though Marcia's costly and unnecessary messing around in town meant he was going to have to deal with this by himself. He was on the way to face it when he heard the words, "Gaius, dear!"

His stepmother was possibly the last person he wanted to see.

"Cook says the boys have been fighting again and the stable lad says you came home without Marcia!"

"The boys are fine," he assured her. "And Marcia's in town with Tilla."

"On her own? How will she get home?"

"Tilla's driving."

"Oh, Gaius!"

"I came home early to inspect the bathhouse floor," he told her, waving the key in the air.

"Are you sure it's safe? Should I come in with you?"

"No!"

"All right, dear. There's no need to be tetchy."

"Sorry," he said. "I'm just worried about this business with Flora."

"Oh, I know. Poor Flora. Verax always seemed such a

nice boy."

Back in the bathhouse poor Flora, no longer naked, glowered at him from one end of the hot room bench. The nice boy, on Ruso's orders, was standing at the other end. His face was blank and he was staring straight at Ruso, which was especially annoying because he was clearly doing it to show off in front of his girl. Wishing he had put them in separate rooms, Ruso said quietly, "You promised not to go near my sister."

"He didn't!" Flora pulled her linen wrap tighter around her shoulders in a belated show of modesty. "It was me."

Ruso ignored her. "Well?"

Verax said nothing.

"It was the boys," Flora continued. "They were hot. They sneaked in to play in the pool."

"My nephews know you're in here too?"

Verax nodded.

This was getting worse by the moment. "What happened? I mean, before—" He gestured towards his sister.

Flora said, "The boys came—"

"I wasn't asking you."

Verax swallowed. "I heard someone come in," he said. "I hid in here and watched through the crack in the door. The boys were playing in the water. Splashing each other. Then after a bit the little one went under and didn't come up, and his brother didn't notice."

"If it wasn't for Verax," Flora declared, "you would have a drowned nephew lying out there at the bottom of the bath."

Verax said, "I told them I wouldn't tell anybody they'd been in here if they promised not to give me away."

Of course the subtlety of this deal had been beyond a five-year-old. The little lad who owed his life to Verax had instantly run to tell Flora that he knew a secret.

"His brother tried to shut him up," Flora explained, "But they were both wet, so it was obvious where they'd been."

Ruso made a mental note to put one of the staff in charge of the boys until their parents came home.

"And then I came over here, and—" She squared her shoulders. "You're so mean, Gaius! You could have told me he was here!"

"This is exactly why I didn't." Ruso turned to Verax. "You'll have to go."

"But we love each other, Gaius!" Flora, flouting the earlier order to *sit in that corner and don't move!* scuttled across to cling to her man as if she were saving him from being dragged away by wild animals. "We'll go together!" she assured him. "We'll go somewhere nobody knows us!"

The wheelwright carried on staring at Ruso with the expression of a man trying to keep his face blank until his mind caught up. "You can find work," Flora persisted, talking to the underside of his chin. "We'll get married and I can look after you!"

At least Verax now had the grace to look embarrassed. Ruso opened his mouth to tell Flora not to be ridiculous, but she had not finished.

"You can't stop us now, Gaius. I might be pregnant. Have you thought of that?"

Ruso, who had indeed thought of that, closed his eyes and let out a long breath that was more weariness than exasperation.

When he opened his eyes, Flora was still looking straight at him. “You’ve got to help us.”

He glared back at her. “I was helping you already,” he told her. “But what I think I’ll do now is turn him in and pack you off to marry somebody with more sense.”

18

It was all very well saying that Verax must be sent back, but quite another thing to make it happen when the family's only vehicle was still in town and wouldn't be back until Marcia had had her fill of pointless pampering. Ruso could march the wheelwright all the way back to Sabinus's estate in chains, but he would need a couple of escorts in case the wretched man tried to make a run for it, and he wasn't sure how far he could rely on any of his own people to back him up: they had known Verax far longer than he had. He could probably borrow a cart from next door, but the last thing he wanted to do was encourage his stepmother's fantasy that he would one day divorce Tilla and marry the attractive and wealthy widow who lived just beyond the olive grove.

Flora, sensing weakness, refused to leave the bathhouse when ordered, even when Ruso threatened to tell her mother what was going on.

"Tell her, then!" retorted Flora, tossing her dishevelled curls. "She'll blame you for letting Verax stay here."

Ruso opened his mouth to tell her not to be ridiculous, then closed it again. She was right.

Meanwhile Verax, demonstrating more good sense than he had earlier, said nothing.

Neither of them deserved to hear any good news, so Ruso said nothing to them about finding out who had murdered Titus. Instead he went outside and told the stable boy to call him as soon as Tilla got back with the cart, and to leave the mules in harness. Then he went straight back to the hot room. He wasn't sure what he was hoping to achieve in there, but he was damned if he was going to reward the young lovers by leaving them alone together.

"I don't see why you want Verax to go back to the estate," Flora announced as soon as he entered. "You promised me you'd sort this out."

Ruso leaned back against the wall and folded his arms. If he tried to drag Flora away, would it end in a fight with a younger man that he might not win? Or would the wheelwright be secretly relieved?

He took a deep breath and straightened up. "I promised I'd do my best for you," he said with what he felt was, in the circumstances, impressive calm. "And that's what I've been doing. So has Tilla. Meanwhile you're behaving in a way that could see you pregnant by a man executed for murder."

Verax lifted his chin. "It's my fault, sir, I—"

"Oh, take no notice of my brother!" Flora shifted along the bench and tugged at Verax's hand, encouraging him to sit down. "It wouldn't be that bad. Everyone knows you can get a baby taken away. Gaius is a doctor: I bet he knows how to do it. Don't you, Gaius?"

Ruso felt his chest tighten. "Nobody knows how to do it safely, you stupid girl!"

"I am not a—"

"Women die!" Ruso snapped. "Of the ones who don't, some of them can never have children afterwards."

"Is that what happened to Tilla? Is that why you had to adopt?"

Verax said, "Flora."

Ruso took a pace towards her. "Get out. Just go away."

"I'm not going until you promise—"

"Out!"

Something in his voice must have told her she had gone too far. She gave a little squeak of alarm and ran for the door, with, "You're so horrible!"

He could hear her sobbing outside.

Verax got to his feet. "I'm ready to go back to the estate now, sir."

"I'm not ready to take you."

"I'll go alone, sir. I'll hand myself in. I give you my word."

"Your word," Ruso told him, "is not worth a great deal."

This time when he locked the door, he took both keys with him and sent someone to fetch the gangly young Briton he had bought in Rome. Even after several weeks in their household the slave—only bought because Tilla felt sorry for him—still spoke next to no Latin. He didn't seem to grasp much of the local language here either, but for once his limitations were useful. Ruso placed him on guard outside the bathhouse, confident that nobody would be able to talk him into abandoning his post.

Flora had disappeared, which was good because her brother did not want to see her any more than she would want to see him. He strode over to the stables, where the lad had finished splitting the wood and was now stacking it in a neat pile against the wall of the furnace room at the back of the bathhouse. Ruso climbed briefly onto the mounting-block to check the front gate and squint at the road beyond. Still no sign of Tilla.

"It's ridiculous a place this size only having one vehicle," he muttered, bending to collect an armful of wood and carry it across to the stack.

The stable lad stood beside him, slotting fresh-cut wood into the gaps in the stack. He had contrived to cut everything to more or less the same length, thus making an impressively neat display that would soon vanish when Ruso ran out of excuses not to fire up the underfloor heating. The lad said, "Verax could have built us another cart, master."

Ruso clapped a chunk of wood on top of the stack and scowled as the pieces beneath it shifted and threatened to fall into disarray.

"He's done lots of repairs on the one we have, master. He's very good."

"Did anyone ask you?"

The lad swallowed and said nothing.

If he had apologized, Ruso might even have considered making an apology himself, but since he didn't, they stacked the rest of the wood in silence. Ruso had only intended to help out with one token armful, but now that he had put the slave in his place more firmly than was necessary, he felt oddly uncomfortable about abandoning him to finish the work on his own. So they tramped back and forth, passing without speaking, while Ruso wondered how long a man could be expected to keep on doing his best in the face of gross ingratitude.

His thoughts were interrupted by a cry of, "Someone's coming!" and then, "Oh my goodness, is that—? Gaius! Gaius, where are you?"

He emerged to see a cloud of dust rising from the

farm track and in front of it, a pair of horses cantering towards them. The carriage bouncing behind them was unfamiliar, but the driver was not.

"What *is* she doing, dear?" his stepmother demanded. "That's not our cart, surely?" When he said nothing she went on, "Is that how they drive where she comes from? Does she think she's in a race?"

The carriage flew over a large bump and Ruso was sure he saw daylight between his wife and the driver's seat. Aware of the stable lad standing beside him, he said, "Whose carriage is it?"

"Those are Publius Germanicus's horses, master."

"Oh, gods above!"

They both ran forward to drag open the gate, Ruso fighting down his fear that it was the horses, and not his wife, who would decide when to stop.

Yet just as the lad said, "Is it true that women drive war chariots in Britannia, master?" Tilla called out something and shifted her hands and the horses slowed to a trot. The nearside wheel missed the gatepost by a couple of inches, the stable lad stepped forward to seize a bridle, and the carriage came to a reasonably controlled halt in the middle of the yard.

"Where is Marcia?" Arria rushed past Tilla and was there as the carriage door swung open. "Marcia! Are you all right, dear? You look terrible! You could have been—whoever is that?"

Tilla grasped one of the ornate metal lions flanking the driver's seat, clambered down and handed the bundled reins to the stable lad. Her hair was wild and her face streaked with dust. "It's Publius's sister," she said. "I brought her as fast as I could, husband. You have to do something."

19

Even though Tilla had told them there was a patient in urgent need of care, none of the people gathering in the yard seemed to be interested. The stepmother was still making a fuss over Marcia, the stable lad was anxiously checking the horses and even her own husband was asking, "Are you all right, Tilla?"

"I am well," she told him, shrugging the stiffness out of her shoulders and flexing fingers that were still gripping invisible reins. "It is Corinna we need to worry about."

"That," Marcia announced, flapping one hand to shoo her mother aside and stepping down from the carriage, "was disgusting." Before Arria could interrupt she went on, "It was just as well we went over to visit her. Their staff are useless. She told them she didn't want a doctor, so they just left her lying on a couch with a jug of wine and some honey-water."

"But dear, why—?"

"Tilla said if we borrowed their carriage it wouldn't be as bumpy, but it was still like being thrown down a mountain. The slave's been holding Corinna on the bucket most of the way. I'm surprised I didn't throw up myself."

In a far corner of the carriage, Corinna was clutching the arm of her slave girl as if she were afraid of toppling over. The girl was holding a bowl covered with a stained cloth, ready to offer it to her mistress at any moment. Corinna looked even worse than when they had set off. Lank hair was stuck to her forehead and her dark eyes were sunk deep into their sockets. Her bloodless lips moved, but no sound came out.

"We are here now," Tilla assured her, placing a hand on the thin shoulder and hoping she had not made a very foolish decision in subjecting the girl to such a journey. "You will be safe with us. We have sent a message to tell your brother where you are, and my husband will help me look after you. He is a very good medicus."

A shadow filled the carriage doorway as her husband climbed in. He introduced himself to the patient, but Corinna showed no sign of noticing or caring.

Flora made surprisingly little complaint when her brother told her she would be giving up her room for Corinna. "And she'll be borrowing some of your clothes." After Corinna was transferred from the carriage one of the staff brought warm water and towels and then everyone was shooed away. Even Corinna's personal maid was sent to wash and find herself some food in the kitchen. At last Tilla and Ruso were alone with their patient.

"You will feel much better when you are clean," Tilla promised, handing Corinna a towel to wipe her mouth and wringing out a wet cloth to wash her. "I will tell my husband the things we talked about, and you can listen and make sure I tell him right, and then we will all decide what to do."

The girl lifted a hand. "Don't tell..."

"We will say nothing to Marcia," Tilla promised. "Nor to—"

"Not again!" Corinna gave a sudden wail and bent forward to clutch at her stomach. "Oh please, please, somebody help me!" She began rocking back and forth, moaning softly.

Tilla gave the girl her hand to grip. "It will pass soon," she promised, hoping she was right, because this was far more like poisoning of the stomach than premature labour, and its course was much harder to predict. Corinna gasped and rolled off the bed, just making it to the bucket in time.

When they finally put her in a clean tunic and lifted her into bed she lay in silence as Tilla told the story.

"Last month," Tilla said, "Corinna found out she was with child. It was not a good thing for her. So she began starving herself and taking hot baths. Her brother noticed she was behaving oddly. She pretended it was grief for their father, but when she did not stop, the arguments started. Then she tried the things many women try: stepping across a viper, and over cyclamen roots, and drinking the wine of... somewhere."

"Keryneia," said her husband. "And she threw herself down the stairs?"

Tilla nodded. "Publius sent her to their country house to recover and someone advised him to give her that resin. Op something."

"Opoponax," he said.

"Didn't work," mumbled Corinna. "Nothing works." She twisted to look up at Ruso. "She says you're a surgeon." Her hand shot up to grasp his wrist and she seemed to be trying to drag him down. "She says you can help me. You must help me!"

“We will help you, Corinna,” he promised.

“Yes! Take it away, now!”

Tilla said, “When the opoponax did not work, she tried—”

“I didn’t know it would be like this!” Corinna began to whimper. “Please. I can’t go on like this.”

“Now she is very sore and...” Tilla gestured towards the girl, who now lay on her side with one arm up over her head, hiding her face. “She is as you see.”

He asked all the questions she had asked herself, and more. Corinna struggled to pay attention and stopped several times to beg him to “take it away”.

Tilla knew what the answer would be. His explanation of why surgery was too dangerous unless her own life was at risk was as kind as it could be, but still unwelcome. When he hurried away to mix up some medicine Corinna, now too weak to sob, lay on the bed and whispered, “Let me die.”

Tilla took one of the cold hands in her own. “Listen to me,” she urged. “This is not worth dying for, do you understand me? You have your whole life in front of you.”

“My life is ruined.”

“No, it is not, Corinna. I promise you. There will be many good things ahead for you.”

The door opened and her husband reappeared. “Thorn-bush root,” he said, holding out a cup. “Lucky we had some.”

He would have said it was lucky whatever it was: healing was about encouraging the patient as well as choosing the right treatment. Tilla held the cup to the girl’s lips and the dull eyes tried to focus on her own.

Corinna mouthed, “Do you promise?”

"Many good things," said Tilla. "I promise."

The girl had just begun to drink when they were interrupted by someone knocking at the door. "Corinna?" called a man's voice. "Are you in there? It's me."

Corinna pushed the cup away and whispered a hoarse, "No."

"It's me, Chubs. What's going on?" The young man Tilla recognized as Publius opened the door anyway, took one look at his sister, and muttered, "Gods above!" He crouched beside her, putting a hand out to touch the lank hair and then withdrawing it. "What have they done to you?"

The head moved from side to side. "You said nobody would want me."

"You—oh, Chubs!" He took the thin hand in his own. "They promised me the medicine was safe!"

"It didn't work. I had to try something else."

"I didn't mean you to do something like this!"

Corinna wriggled closer to him and whispered, "I am so sorry."

"I know."

"I thought he liked me."

"Shh!" he urged her. "Not now." He looked up at Ruso. "You're a medicus. Do something."

Tilla passed him the cup. "This will help her. We are lucky there was some in the medicine box."

She watched as Corinna made another effort to drink with her brother's help. Then she heard a movement behind her. Verax was standing in the doorway. Nobody else noticed him until he said, "Sir?"

Publius glanced over his shoulder and then turned to Ruso. "What's he doing here?"

Tilla was startled by the sharpness of Ruso's "He thinks he's going to marry my sister."

Publius said, "Oh," and turned back to Corinna. "Everything will be all right, Chubs. I won't let anyone hurt you."

Verax coughed, and said, "Sir, I can see you're busy. I'll go back to the estate now."

Ruso said, "Yes," and turned back to the patient. In the presence of such a sick young woman, what Flora's boyfriend did or didn't do was not important. But Publius still took the time to say, "Sorry about having you locked up the other night. It's all sorted out now. I've spoken to Sabinus and told him it was the girl who did it. That's why she lied."

Instead of leaving, Verax stood in the doorway looking confused.

Ruso said, "Just clear off, will you?" and they were alone again with Corinna and her anxious brother.

Resting his head against hers, Publius murmured, "You should have sent for me."

"You were angry."

"I'm not angry now."

The girl closed her eyes and Publius mouthed to Ruso, "Is she still...?"

Ruso looked at Tilla, who whispered, "I think so." Babies were often much harder to dislodge than people thought.

Publius raised the medicine cup again.

"You are doing very well," Tilla told her before turning to the brother. "Did you say you have been to tell Sabinus that the girl Xanthe killed his son?"

"Yes."

"What will happen to her?"

Publius shifted to sit next to his sister, stretching his long legs out on the bed. "Sabinus will deal with it."

"What will he do?"

Ruso looked up. "It's no concern of ours, wife."

Publius said, "He's going to hire someone to look for her."

"And when they catch her? Will there be a trial?"

"They won't catch her," Publius told her. "A girl like that can easily disappear. Change her name, move to a different town. She's not like a decent girl with family connections."

"But what if they do?"

"My wife liked her," Ruso explained.

Publius sighed. "We all liked her," he said.

Tilla got to her feet. "Will you watch your sister for a moment? I need to talk to my husband."

20

They were in the study that looked out over the vineyard. The sort of room where Roman men hid so they could think about important things without being interrupted. As far as Tilla could tell, Roman women did not have studies. Perhaps because they could think about important things and work at the same time, or perhaps because the things they thought about were not considered important. But now there were two things that must be spoken of in private.

She pushed the door firmly closed behind her. The first thing had happened before she and her husband met. Neither of them had even mentioned it again since the day she had told him about it and she had thought it was settled, but now... "Did you refuse Corinna because of what happened to me?"

He frowned, "Did you want me to say yes to her? Put her in the danger you went through in the hands of that—whoever she was?"

She said, "When I see all those children your brother has, I think perhaps you are disappointed in me."

For a moment he did not answer. Then he moved closer and cupped his hands around her face. "Do you seriously think," he said, "that I want to live like my brother?"

"You are happy with Mara?"

"I'm happy with Mara. If we want more, we'll adopt them."

She said, "I am a lucky woman."

"I like to think so."

"I am much more lucky than Xanthe."

He drew back, releasing her. "Did you bring me in here to talk about Xanthe?"

"That is the other thing." She leaned back against the door so he could not escape. "Listen to me, husband. I do not want an argument, but that young man was not killed by Xanthe."

"What? Tilla, this really isn't the time to—"

"If Xanthe had done it, she would make up a better lie."

"Maybe she's not a very good liar," he told her. "I know you liked her, but people saw her with Ti—"

"There is more," she said. "I told you I was there when Publius's man was leaving her house. I heard what the doorman said to him. It was, *Tell your master he can rely on Xanthe*. What do you think that means?"

He said, "Who knows? Maybe Publius can rely on her turning up to the next party now she's been paid. We ought to get back."

Tilla felt a stab of doubt. "Anyway," she said, raising her chin, "now Xanthe has run away with the doorman and some money."

"Exactly as Publius predicted. She's on the run because she killed Titus."

"No. I think she was paid to tell a lie and run away."

"Then she deserves to get the blame," he said. "Can we discuss this later?"

"If Sabinus's man catches her you know what will happen. She will not get a trial. She will be dragged into an alley and have her throat cut. Because people say Xanthe is not a decent girl. And that is what is at the bottom of all this."

He looked her over as if he was assessing a patient. "Are you sure you don't want an argument?"

"Corinna is a decent girl with a family. "But she is also single and pregnant."

He sighed. "Wife, it's no good expecting me to guess what you're talking about."

"Publius sent to Xanthe and her friends a while ago asking for remedies to get rid of an unwanted baby. Ask him who the father of Corinna's baby is."

"Why can't I ask you? Or her?"

"She won't tell me. But I think it is Titus. I think Publius was the one with a reason to be angry with Titus, not Xanthe. And this morning Publius sent his man to pay Xanthe to tell a lie."

He scratched his ear with one finger: something he often did when he was thinking. "Why would he do that?"

"I do not know. But Publius said just now, that is why she lied. How did he know Xanthe lied? Did you tell him?"

"No."

He was not looking as impressed as she had expected. "What is the matter? It all makes sense! Even Flora said Titus used to flirt with lots of girls."

He slumped back against the desk. "Don't talk to me about Flora. I just caught her and the boyfriend stark naked in the bathhouse."

"Really?" She could not resist a smile, but that seemed to make him even more grim-faced. "Oh husband, they are going to marry anyway! What did you expect? What were you like at that age?"

Instead of replying, he pointed in the direction of the room where they had left the ailing Corinna. "I'm not having my sister end up like that."

She placed a hand on his arm. "Flora will not end up like that. She has chosen a much better man. Now stop sulking and tell me, am I right about Publius and Titus?"

"I hope not."

"I know it is more bad news for Corinna, but—"

"It's bad news for us, too," he said. "We owe Publius more money than you can imagine. What do you think he'll do if he knows we suspect him of murder?"

"But am I right?"

He shook his head. "Just leave it be, Tilla. We've done what we said we'd do: Verax is free to marry my sister, which I suppose I'll have to agree to—"

"What about Xanthe?"

"Xanthe's gone off with a man and a pile of money, and the Empire is a very big place to hide in." He pushed himself off the desk. "Sometimes, wife, you just have to let things go."

21

The day was fading by the time the worst seemed to be over for Corinna. Ruso left her asleep in Flora's bed, being watched over by her own slave and by Tilla. He and Publius retreated to the haven of the study, where Publius sank onto the couch and put his head in his hands. "All that for nothing," he muttered when Ruso told him there was no sign of a miscarriage so far. "And you won't do it?"

"If it were to save her life," Ruso said, pushing open the shutters to reveal the evening sun slanting through the vines and wishing he didn't have to have this conversation. "I'd risk it. But it's not the pregnancy that's put her in danger. It's the things she's done to try and end it."

Publius shook his head and muttered, "You have no idea."

"I suppose there's no point in speaking to the father?"

The silence that followed was broken only by the chirrup of the cicadas and the distant laughter of children: one of them the nephew who would have drowned today if Verax had not been there to save him.

Ruso said, "You're welcome to stay here tonight. I'll get some food brought in if you don't want to face my family."

"Thanks."

At the moment all they could do for Corinna was to offer her more thorn-root and a safe place to recuperate. Perhaps a safe place was what Publius needed too. He could not be more than eighteen or nineteen years of age: young to be plunged into running the sort of complex family affairs that must accompany the name and the wealth of a Germanicus. If, just as he had shouldered these responsibilities, a so-called friend had seduced his younger sister...

Ruso leaned on the windowsill, but the vineyard had ceased to be a relaxing view ever since he had spotted the fugitive Verax out there. The more he thought about it, the more likely it seemed that Tilla was right about the murder. And the less likely it seemed that Publius would ever admit it. The blame would rest with Xanthe, who had taken a bribe and fled. It wasn't ideal, as Tilla had pointed out, but neither was picking an unnecessary battle with a man to whom your family owed a great deal of money.

His attention was caught by a pale shape weaving an unsteady course along the stone path below the window. A dead moth, its wings partly extended, was being carried by a crowd of ants. When they approached a gap between the stones the ants turned the moth this way and that, trying different approaches until they found one that took it safely across.

The ants that were not carrying the moth seemed to be urging their comrades on and occasionally stepping in to help. They all gave the impression of being excited about their one task and agreed on their direction of travel.

If only a human family could form such a willing and co-operative—

He stepped away from the window. A man had sunk to worrying depths if he found himself jealous of a colony of ants.

Someone was approaching along the corridor. He felt his stomach tense. The sound of footsteps faded, and he let out a long breath. In here, for the moment, there was peace.

Beyond the study walls, two women were in trouble. One of them was a "decent" girl with a loving brother: the other a prostitute whom he'd never met, but who seemed to be considered dispensable to everyone who knew her—except his own wife.

Despite what he had said to Tilla, Ruso was still torn between searching for a tactful way of asking who Corinna's lover was, and not wanting to know. If it really was Titus, then the murderer was sitting barely six feet away with his head bowed and his hair sticking up between his fingers. Meanwhile the relatively innocent Xanthe, duped into making herself look guilty, was in danger of being murdered herself. And Ruso had unwittingly been part of the deception.

The fate of Corinna, no matter how you saw it, was pitiful. It was not hard to imagine the arguments between her and her brother once he had found out the reason for her strange behaviour. No doubt, in the heat of the moment, he had been angry with her. No doubt he had said things that had caused her to despair. Because Corinna was not a girl who could vanish from one town and reappear in another to make a fresh start. While Xanthe earned a living by selling herself, a wealthy heiress was a commodity for others to set out on a stall in the marriage market, and since the death of their father it was Publius's job to get the best deal for her that he could. It was all very well for Tilla to smile indulgently and say, "They are going to marry anyway!" For Corinna and her brother, an unwanted pregnancy would make a satisfactory deal much harder to come by.

Ruso closed the shutters in case anyone passing should overhear, and remarked into the gloom, "If I were to find out someone had been bedding my sister behind my back, I'd be furious."

No response.

"Especially if he was someone I trusted."

"I'd be angry with her, as well," Ruso went on. "For not having more sense." *I might even be angry enough to tell her nobody else would want her*. But not now that he had seen the damage such words could do. Now he wanted to run after Flora and tell her it was all right: that as long as she was healthy and happy he really didn't care what she got up to. Within reason.

He heard his guest shift on the couch.

"I would expect the man to own up to his responsibilities."

Finally Publius said, "He laughed. He said it might not be his, how could anybody know?"

Ruso tried to imagine his own fury if Verax had said something like that about Flora. It was worryingly easy. Hesitantly, not wanting to push too far, he said, "I'd want to—" He was interrupted by a knock on the door. "I'm busy!"

"Master, it's two men for Master Publius. They've brought our cart back and they've come to collect his carriage and they want to know if he's going home in it or if they should leave now while there's still some light."

Publius called, "Tell them I'll be home tomorrow." As the footsteps faded away down the corridor he added,

"You were about to ask if it was me who killed Titus."

Ruso was conscious of taking a breath before he spoke. "Was it?"

"Are you hoping to blackmail me into cancelling your loan?"

"I'm not sure what I'm doing, to be honest. I know that if I were you, I would have wanted to kill him."

Publius said, "I've been trying to sort this out ever since Corinna told me. It just gets worse. I only wanted to shut him up. I truly didn't mean to..." His voice died away.

Ruso waited.

"They were all over the house," Publius continued softly. "Wrecking things. As if they didn't care. I warned Titus to clear off. He told me not to spoil everyone's fun. He gave me the wine jug and told me to calm down. I was so angry that I—" He paused. "I keep trying to make things right. But everything I do makes it worse. When the kitchen maid said she'd seen the driver standing over the body, I thought the gods had sent me a way out. I mean, he was only a slave!"

Ruso said nothing.

"Then I found out he was Titus's brother. Because of me, poor old Sabinus was going to lose both sons at once. But I couldn't confess, could I? I had Corinna to look after. So I thought if I made it clear that my girl never actually saw who did it, Sabinus was bound to send somebody round asking questions. And I paid Xanthe a lot of money to lie about Verax and then disappear. I guessed she wouldn't know enough to be convincing."

"That was a risk."

"I could hardly expect her to knowingly incriminate herself, could I?"

"And you got your friends to say she'd been seen with Titus just before his death."

"They were too drunk to know what was going on. Everyone was supposed to blame her and then you wouldn't need to save Verax and you wouldn't ask any more awkward questions."

Ruso said, "You should have spoken to Titus's father."

"And discuss my sister's honour with somebody else? Titus was supposed to be a friend. I thought he would do the right thing."

"You'd really have wanted your sister married to Titus?"

"He was set to inherit the estate. She liked him. He could be fun. It would have been a good alliance."

Suddenly the simple wheelwright son of a slave seemed to Ruso like every matchmaker's dream.

Publius sighed. "It's the funeral tomorrow. I suppose I'll have to go."

"Yes."

"I made one mistake, Ruso. In the heat of the moment."

"Yes."

"So I suppose the question is, are you and I going to ruin each other over one mistake?"

22

Ruso was beginning to think that having a study wasn't such a good idea after all. As soon as a man retreated to be alone with his thoughts, people knew exactly where to find him. Not that he was thinking: anything was better than dwelling on the memory of Titus's funeral pyre this afternoon, so he was doing his best to distract himself. A battered scroll of Dioscorides' advice on medicines lay on the desk in front of him, weighted down at one end by an inkwell and at the other end by a small bowl that now held only a scatter of nutshells and pastry crumbs. He was almost at the end of a passage about the properties of wine made with seawater froth—unsurprisingly, the great man deemed it useless in either sickness or health—when there was yet another knock on the door.

All Dioscorides' previous interrupters—Ruso's stepmother needing money to pay the cushion-maker, a farm hand seeking approval for a decision, and a neighbour asking him to remove a dried bean from a small girl's ear—had apologized for disturbing him.

Tilla, striding in with Mara perched on her right hip, did not bother. "Flora says," she announced, "that Verax went to the funeral."

He lifted his forefinger from the cramped text and immediately lost his place. "Titus was his brother," he said, knowing this was not what she had come to discuss.

His offer to take the baby was ignored, so he indicated that his wife might like to sit on the couch. The couch was ignored too. Instead, Tilla leaned back against the closed door so there was no escape, and said, "She says Verax heard that Xanthe is dead."

"Yes. I'm sorry."

"You knew this?"

He settled into what he would always think of as his father's chair and tipped some crumbs into his hand so Mara could help herself. "Sabinus told everyone at the funeral. The man he hired to find her conveniently came across her body just outside town."

"The man murdered her."

"It sounds that way," he said, watching his daughter's small fingers pick out a crumb with impressive precision.

"Were you thinking of telling me?"

"Of course." It was true. He had been thinking of telling her, and then thinking of ways he might avoid it. He was certainly not going to mention the way Publius had turned pale at the news.

"You know Xanthe did not kill anyone. All she did was tell a lie because that Publius asked her to."

Ruso considered rephrasing this as, *She took a bribe to incriminate an innocent man*, and decided it would not help.

"So," his wife continued. "What will you do?"

He said, "The same as I've done until now. Nothing."

"Nothing?"

"Nothing."

Mara's dark head turned from one parent to the other. Plainly she sensed the tension even though she did not understand the words.

Tilla said, "I do not understand."

Ruso, not entirely sure he understood himself, busied himself brushing the last crumbs off his hands.

"In return are you hoping Publius will do nothing about the money your family owes him?"

"He offered to forget the loan," he said. "Naturally I refused to accept."

The eyes that were the colour of the sea opened wide and stared into his own. For once, his wife was lost for words.

"It would be like taking a bribe for silence," he explained.

Tilla pursed her lips, and he resisted the urge to keep talking.

"Already," she said, "you are doing one wrong thing. I do not know why you cannot hold your nose and do another one."

He took his time rolling up the scroll, gently tapping the ends so that the edges were neatly aligned.

"Are you going to tell your brother you have thrown away this money your family could have saved?"

"Probably not." Absolutely not.

She watched while he slid the scroll back into the leather case, then said, "Is it true that Publius is going all the way to Egypt to join a legion?"

"The Third Cyrenaica," he told her. "He knows someone who can recommend him for a tribune's post. He'll take Corinna with him."

"And is it true that Egypt is even hotter than here?"

"Yes."

"Ugh," she said. Then she added, "But it is a long way away. They can tell people the baby's father died, and nobody will need to know the rest."

"I'm glad you approve."

"I am very sad for Corinna."

He said, "I'm sad for both of them."

"There is no need to look at me like that," she said.

"Like what?"

"I too will do nothing and say nothing, because telling the truth will bring worse trouble to Corinna."

"I hadn't really thought of that," he confessed.

"Also," she added, "if your brother finds out what you have done about that money, neither of us will be welcome here ever again."

23

By the afternoon of the next day Corinna was feeling well enough to enjoy a little sunshine in the garden. Mara was indoors taking a nap, so Tilla settled Corinna on cushions in the wicker chair and then joined Marcia and Flora on the bench under the dappled shade of the pergola. Flora was prattling on happily about wedding plans while at the same time complaining that her mother would drive her mad fussing over every detail.

"Now you know what I had to put up with," Marcia told her.

"And then I suppose it'll be, when are you going to have a baby?"

Neither of them had been told why Corinna was ill and obviously Flora had not guessed. Tilla glanced across at her patient, who was leaning back with her eyes closed. "Are you comfortable here, Corinna?" she asked, wishing they would talk of something else. "We can go inside if you are too hot."

Corinna shook her head. "This is a lovely garden."

Was it? Tilla narrowed her eyes against the glare and surveyed the cracked and empty fountain basin. The ancient pergola that looked as though only the vine around it was stopping it from falling on their heads. There was nothing in the weedy flower beds that you could eat, and only one thing you could use for medicine, and the air throbbed with the screech of insects that sounded as if they were being shut in a door... but Corinna was right. If you closed your eyes and inhaled, the scent drifting across from the purple lavender filled you with wonder. And with sadness, because although Corinna was still alive to enjoy it, Xanthe would never again feel the warmth of the sun on her skin, nor hear the drone of the bees as they went about their work.

Publius had avenged his sister's abandonment by killing Titus, and then sacrificed Xanthe to escape punishment. Even Tilla had agreed to do nothing more about it. Even Tilla, who had met Xanthe and liked her, was now guilty of acting as if one young woman deserved justice more than another.

The whole thing had been about honour, but it was hard to find any honourable part of it. Apart, perhaps, from her husband's refusal to accept payment for his silence. And now they were hiding that as if it were a guilty secret.

Her eyes opened at a shout from the direction of the gate, followed by the cries of children. Flora broke off from whatever she was saying and said, "They aren't fighting again, are they?"

"Leave it to the staff," said Marcia. "If there's no blood, there's no need to get involved. And if there is, we'll send Gaius."

"It does not sound like fighting." Tilla stood up and shaded her eyes. "It is your brother come home!"

It was an echo of their own arrival a few days ago. Lucius and his wife were barely inside the gates when their children raced up to greet them. The slaves carried the bags to the house while small voices competed to be heard.

"I nearly drowned in the water!"

"The boys stole my oil flask and put beetles in it!"

"He nearly knocked my eye out, look!"

"I have missed you all!" Their mother was dragged down into a forest of clutching arms while the solid form of their father paused by the gate to survey the scene, his expression hidden by the shade of his straw hat.

Tilla was surprised to see a hand reaching towards her over the tops of the children's heads. "Tilla! I have something for you."

The cries turned to, "What about us?" "Have we got presents?" and "What have we got?"

"In a moment. I need to speak with Tilla first."

"But have we?"

"Wait and see." She reached into her bag and a shimmer of yellow silk billowed out on the breeze.

Tilla reached up and caught a corner. The silk rippled out above the children like a banner.

"We met a young woman just now," said her sister-in-law. "Up where the track turns off the main road. She said to give you this and to say she was sorry."

Tilla fingered the delicate fabric. There was the hole where it had caught on the nail. "To me?"

"A blond girl. Very pretty. Only wearing one earring. She said you would know who she was."

"She was on the main road? Just now? You spoke to her?"

"She wanted to say goodbye. She is going on a long journey."

"But—"

"A man was driving her in a little two-wheel carriage. Do you know—"

But Tilla was gone, hitching up her skirts and racing

away up the farm track in a hopeless bid to catch a vehicle that was no more than a smudge of dust on the horizon.

24

It was late. Lucius had retreated into the study to think about farm business while his wife put the children to bed. The stable lad had gone to join the other slaves in the bunkhouse after working like a dog for most of the afternoon to keep the bathhouse fire going, because apparently the return of Lucius and his wife really was a special occasion. Now Ruso was alone in a room filled with wavering shadows cast by the one lamp he had propped on the side of the bath. He took a deep breath and then lowered himself until the water closed over his head.

Earlier this evening he had taken Corinna home to the town house, where Publius had run to embrace her and begged her never to do anything as silly as that ever again. While the staff hurried her off to her own bed, Ruso and Publius had held a private conversation that left Publius in tears and Ruso convinced that he was doing the right thing.

Tilla had been less certain. Standing in their bedroom and streaming the yellow silk through a small circle formed between her thumb and forefinger, she said, "If this rich boy thinks he can use ordinary people like he used Verax and Xanthe, and nothing bad will happen, will he not grow up to do more wicked things?"

"He might," Ruso conceded. "Or he might have

learned that he needs to use power responsibly."

Tilla said, "Hmph," and swirled the silk in the air so it floated down and moulded itself to the shape of her hand.

"Besides," Ruso added, "he was right: Xanthe really did find a way to escape and start again."

"He did not deserve to know that."

"Perhaps."

"So why tell him?"

"Because," he said, "a while ago, you asked me if I could remember what I was like at that age. And I can."

Tilla wriggled her fingers and watched the silk ripple. "If we are telling truths," she said, "perhaps I should tell you that Titus was worse than we knew."

"Really?"

"He really did lay hands on Flora. She told me today. It was after Verax had warned him to leave her alone. She fought him off, but she was too frightened to say anything in case Verax did something bad to him."

"Does Verax know now?"

"She says not. I promised her we would not tell him."

Ruso reached forward and lifted the covering of silk off his wife's hand. "Lying to her husband is not a good way to start their marriage."

"You think telling him she has kept a secret about another man would be better?"

"She should have said something to the family at the time! Why didn't she tell Lucius? For all we know, warning Titus off might have saved Corinna."

Tilla flung the silk aside. "Promise me you will never, ever say anything like that to her!"

"Of course not, but—"

"I expect," she had continued, "she said nothing

because she knew Lucius would make a big fuss and be cross with her instead of with Titus, just like you are!"

He really did lay hands on Flora.

Ruso shot up out of the water and gasped in air. What would have been wrong with making a fuss? He remembered the delicate features of the dead Titus below the wreath of flowers and he felt his fists tighten. Someone should have done something.

Publius had made a fuss. Publius had done something.

Ruso groped for a towel, rubbed the water out of his eyes and carried the lamp through into the hot room. He set the lamp on the bench and checked the temperature of the heated wall with the back of his hand before leaning against it.

Flora had done what she thought was best. They all had. Now he must make himself think about happier things. About Mara, with her toothy grin and her little fat legs. About Lucius being home to take over the farm. About there being a wedding celebration to arrange. About the warmth of the wall soaking into his skin. About—

His thoughts were interrupted by the squeak of a hinge and the clack of wooden bath sandals across tile.

"Your brother is looking for you." Tilla seated herself beside him. "He wants to know what is the matter with the floor in here."

Ruso groaned. He foresaw future generations of suspicious bathers regularly checking the hot-room floor, even though none of them knew what might be wrong with it.

Tilla said, "I am not sorry I was cross."

"I wasn't angry *with* Flora," he told her. "I was angry

for her."

She said, "I know."

He stretched out his legs, put his hands behind his head and gazed at the dim shapes of painted dolphins plunging across the walls. "One murder," he said, "two false accusations, a dangerous stone fight and a near-drowning in the bathing pool."

"It has been a busy time."

"Yesterday the sister of one of our creditors nearly died under our roof."

"And you have turned down a kind offer to forget a big loan."

"On the other hand," he observed, "I've been kissed by Flora's boyfriend, young love has been consummated on this very bench, and nobody was wrongly executed after all."

"It seems to me," said Tilla, "that your brother chose a very good time to go away."

Ruso shrugged. "For all I know, it could be like this all the time here."

"I hope not."

"I'm never here long enough to tell."

"We are never anywhere for very long, husband." She laid her head on his shoulder. "Are we?"

Whatever he might have said was interrupted by the crash of the outer door opening and his brother calling, "Gaius? Gaius! What's all this nonsense about the floor?"

Ruso said in a low voice, "Are you saying you want to stay here?"

"Gaius, where—ah, there you are! What were you thinking, letting the boys play in here? Flora says if Verax hadn't been here they'd have drowned. And little Lucius is lucky he didn't lose his eye!"

“I don’t want to stay *here*,” Tilla whispered.

Ruso said, “Thank the gods for that.” Then, turning his attention to his brother, he said, “Let me tell you about this chap in Britannia. You’ll never believe what happened to his bathhouse floor...”

Author's Note

Any attempt to "do as the Romans do"—or to write about what they might have done—runs into the question: *which Romans?* Ruso and Tilla exist in a society riven with deep divisions – or as we might see it, social injustice. While those at the top feasted on the fruits of an extensive Empire, a large proportion of the population did not own even their own bodies.

Slavery was not based on race, and was not always forever. A lucky slave who did well might hope for freedom one day, and perhaps for descendants who would inherit the full rights of Roman citizens. In the meantime, slaves' welfare depended largely upon the whim of their owners. There were a few restrictions: Hadrian's ruling that slaves should only be tortured for evidence if they could reasonably be expected to know something about a case was one of them. Until that point, when a serious crime had been committed, the whole household staff might be subjected to the questioners. Hadrian's pronouncement, of course, was carefully framed so as not to impinge upon the "rights" of owners. We might view it as squirming: he probably saw it as a sensible compromise.

The social rules of Tilla's people in Britannia are harder to pin down. We know that British women could rule tribes in their own right (not just as the wives of kings), which suggests a level of equality that their Roman sisters did not enjoy. However, finds of slave chains in non-Roman contexts suggest that at the bottom of society, things were tough wherever you were.

Finally, in case anyone's wondering: Ruso's professional advice is entirely based on what he believes is best for his patients in the light of his medical knowledge. It's unlikely that anything he's asked to do in the course of this story would have been illegal until at least a century later.

Acknowledgements

A novella seems to need just as large a backup team as a full-length book and I'm grateful to Helen Baggott for editing, Alison Samuels for checking the Latin, Bruce Aiken for another wonderful cover, and Araminta Whitley and Marina de Pass for encouragement, advice, technical help, admin and general good sense.

Bill Wahl, Ernesto Spinelli, the excellent Writers in a Café and the Barnstaple WIP group were all kind enough to read and make suggestions, and Andy Downie has nobly battled through so many incarnations of this story that he now has no idea which is the final version.

About the author

Ruth Downie is the author of the New York Times bestseller MEDICUS and a further seven full-length novels in the Gaius Petreius Ruso series. She lives in the south-west of England with a husband, two cats and an unknown number of badgers down a hole in the garden. When she's not writing, many of her happiest moments are spent wielding an archaeological trowel.

Find out more at www.ruthdownie.com